Laurie Depp

consequences...

Secrets, lies and videotape

A division of Hachette Children's Book

First published in Great Britain in 2008
by Hodder Children's Books

1

A Catalogue record for this book is available from the British Library

ISBN-13: 978 0 340 93042 7

Typeset in Baskerville by Avon DataSet Ltd,
Bidford-on-Avon, Warwickshire

Printed in Great Britain by
Clays Ltd, St Ives plc

The paper and board used in this paperback by Hodder Children's
Books are natural recyclable products made from wood grown
in sustainable forests. The manufacturing processes conform to the
environmental regulations of the country of origin.

Prologue

Dawn. Tight camera angle overhead shot. Single bed in small room. Old carpet. Faded posters, thin curtains. There is a young man in bed, shifting restlessly. Cut to close-up. Man's face is sweating, his eyes flickering back and forth. Internal dialogue begins.

The cops are coming for me. I know it. Or maybe worse. Maybe thickset men with overcoats and scars. I look at the clock.

My clock doesn't tick. It doesn't even tock. It hums. It's a cheap plastic thing from Asda, or possibly Lidl. Mum always shops at Asda or Lidl. Or at least she used to when I was small, dragging me behind as I squealed and flailed my limbs like a rebellious octopus.

When I was older Mum made me go alone while she sat staring out the kitchen window, smoking Lucky Strike and looking out for my dad who went to the newsagent one day and never came home again. I gave in to her shopping demands more easily once I'd grown up a bit and realised why she was so sad. By then I'd had to put my octopus days behind me.

'Bry, pop down to Lidl, will ya, love? We need milk.'

'We need bread.'

'We need fish fingers.'

'We need dog food.'

Here's a clue, Mum. Write all this stuff down on a piece of paper during the week and I'll go and get them all at once on a Sunday morning when everyone else is asleep. I'll get up when the humming of the clock becomes too much and begins to remind me of dentist's drills. Shopping lists, Mum, that's the way forward. That's the current programme.

And while we're at it, here's another clue for you. My name's not Bry, or Bryan. Not any more. Not since I escaped. My name's Dan, though I can't tell you that. I can't tell you about the shopping list thing either. If you didn't ask me to go and get you something every five minutes, we'd have nothing to talk about at all. You'd never speak. You'd just smoke yourself into a big lump of nicotine and we'd not realise it was you and we'd throw you into the wheelie bin one Tuesday night saying, 'Anyone seen Mum? She was here just now next to that big lump of brown stuff.'

I look at the clock in question slowly taking shape, as the dim October light squeezes into my boxy room through the chink in the curtains. 8.36 a.m. The early starters will be in the office now, turning on their Macs, rubbing sore heads and talking about which club they were at last night and how many WKDs Rashid had had and how cheesy were those tunes? *That DJ must have been John Peel's dad!* I wished I were there with them, feeling seedy and tired but happy.

They'd be opening their emails now-ish and they'd see the one from the editing suite. The one titled Liarliar.mpg. They'd be clicking on it now. Quicktime would start up. They'd be watching the opening credits, jazzy, funky, state of the art. Then they'd see my face. My calm, apologetic face. Explaining what I'd done.

The light, too pale to be called a glow, illuminates the posters of footballers I no longer support and pop stars I no longer listen to. Not since things started to happen for me in London, not since I changed, since I took control and then lost it again.

In films, where the hero is defusing a bomb, the clock always ticks, even when it's the digital sort that James Bond always stops with 007 seconds left to spare. Either the countdown is ended by cutting the red wire, or possibly the blue one after the hero has changed his mind at the last minute; or else the bomb goes off. Either way the ticking stops.

But in the real world. In my world. Back here in Humsville. In Humdrumsville, the clock never stops; it just keeps on going, keeps on humming.

Even when the thing happens today. Even when they all find out what I've done. Even when they've all watched the movie file. Even when the smelly stuff hits the whirly thing. Life will go on, here at least. Which is why I came back. Why I ran home, back to Mummy. Because let's get real here, no one's going to die. For all the black dread I feel in my gut, no one's going to be killed, or even hurt. Not physically anyway.

And I'll be safe, and warm. And I'll have food to put in the black void inside me. Even when they come for me and start asking questions, and I tell them the truth.

Because surely I can't tell any more lies. I just know that if I tell one more lie the world will end, though the clock will keep humming.

I'll just tell them the truth, and it'll all come out, and Mum will be angry, but it'll fade in time. Like it always does. And then everything will be back to normal. I'm sure of it.

I think I'm sure.

But I'm getting ahead of myself. I need to tell you all sorts of lead-up things before we get to now. I need to tell you about my life so far, about me. Because you won't understand why I did what I did until you know more about me, about who I am. And once you know all the important things, then you'll forgive me. You might even think, 'Hey, I'd have done the same thing.'

No more time-wasting, the clock's humming. So here goes.

Me first. I'm nineteen. Though only just. When the story I'm about to tell you started, I was nearly a year younger. And I think maybe about a hundred years more innocent. It started with a girl of course. It sounds like an old detective film when I say it like that but it's true. In detective films there's always a beautiful girl who ends up being a right cow. Sometimes she turns out to be evil, sometimes good, but either way she screws things up for the Detective, who, let's face it, is usually pretty screwed-up to start with.

In my case there were three beautiful girls to screw me around, four if you count Jen. A regular witches' coven. They weren't really evil of course, none of them. But still, they screwed me around. It wasn't entirely their fault. It was mine for letting them.

But let's start with the first girl. The one who made me think about what I was like and the one who made me think that I didn't like so much what I was like. If that makes sense. Read it again if you don't get it.

What I was like was pretty dull. But nice, definitely nice. That's what all the girls say about me. And funny, that's what all the guys say about me. I was the kind of guy fathers wanted their daughters to bring home, if they had to bring someone home at all. Mothers wanted to give me cake. Grannies wanted to pinch my cheek.

I'm OK looking, but too clean, too smiley, too *nice.* Boy-band instead of Franz Ferdinand. I try for emo but my hair straightens itself and my clothes self-iron. And it's hard to keep your street cred when your mates spot you in Superdrug buying tampons for your mum.

I was, am, a good son. My mother doesn't smile much these days. She can't help it. I had to look after her. Plus my gran is sick, she came to live with us when Dad left and she got sick soon after. I had to help her with stuff, but I don't want to go into details there. I did a lot of fetching. I ran a lot of errands; I did a lot of chores. It was like living in the little house on the prairie, without so many pinafores.

I never had too much time for girls, until I left school and went to college. At least then I could pretend I had to stay late in the editing suite, or go out with my treasured camcorder for a project. What girls I did have time for just wanted to be friends with me. They didn't want to ruin the friendship by sleeping with me. It would get too awkward, they'd say.

'It might not,' I'd reply, limply.

'It always does,' they'd say, shaking their heads in sorrow. *Computer says no.*

Always? I mean, how many times had they tried it to have worked this out? Had they hooked up with all their male friends only to find that it had ruined the friendship? If so, one more wouldn't hurt, surely? Get back on the horse, girls, don't accept failure so easily. Maybe you're just doing it wrong, practise on me.

I was a good friend. A strong, fabric-softened shoulder to cry on, a well-scrubbed ear to cry into. Oh and I'm supposed to be clever, that's what my teachers said, though I was never interested much in school; it wasn't until I had to choose what to look at in college that I thought much about the academic world. I chose Film because I supposed you'd get to watch lots of films. And that there might be girls watching these films too, and that I could talk to them about the films afterwards. And then we could like go and get a coffee, or something. After the film.

I was right on all these things but the girls turned out to be more interested in the films than they were in me. And the rec coffee was horrible. If the college girls I met showed any interest in boys it tended to be the hideously old lecturers or else the hard-drinking, car-driving bad boys from the university who dumped them quickly and regularly, leaving me to pick up the pieces and waste too many Friday nights wringing out tear-soaked hankies and making endless cups of hot chocolate. I never want to watch *Lost in Translation* again. *But it was our film! He said I was prettier than Scarlett!*

Film in general, though, I liked. I soon found that I wanted to be on the other side of the lens. I wanted to be making my own movies. I took my cheap hand-held camera and started pointing it at my mates.

I filmed weeping girls complaining bitterly about the guys that had just dumped them. I made edited video tapes and would show them the results a week or so later when they decided to go back to Dane, or Ryan, or whichever meathead they'd decided they were hopelessly in love with that week.

'See? This is what will happen if you take him back. Sleep with me instead,' I'd say.

'Oh Bryan, you're so funny.'

It never worked, they'd always go back to the bad boys, and I'd always pick up the pieces.

'No I'm not gay, Mum,' I'd say every once in a while when the subject came up. 'I just haven't found the right girl.' And it wasn't that I'd had no experience at all of the opposite sex. It was just that I didn't feel I'd had enough.

And none of the girls ever thought I was the right guy.

Then I met Lucy. She catwalked her way across the quad one day as I sat fiddling with my camera.

I was grumpy that day. Mum had asked me if I could pick up some dry-cleaning for her on my way home. I'd been intending to go hang out with some of the guys after college, but when I hesitated, she put on that tired 'your-father's-left-me' look and I couldn't say no. I hate that look. It's like she's blaming me, as a man, for Dad's going. I didn't make him leave. I didn't suggest he hook up with some tart over the Internet. I was against the idea. Why blame me?

I flipped the camera lens up towards Lucy as she walked and pressed record. I had been experimenting with surreptitious recording, it's the only way you can get people to feel comfortable enough to open up sometimes. But they sometimes go a bit postal when they find out afterwards. But it's a price you have to pay as an *artiste*. Being a brilliant director isn't just pointing your 3G phone at something and pressing the green button.

Lucy walked with confidence. She had something I'd never seen before. It wasn't just that she was tall and more beautiful than Uma Thurman, it was her walk, the way she carried herself. She had me spellbound. I hardly noticed that she was walking straight towards me. It was like a scene from a classy film, shot so well it seemed inevitable. My iPod played 'I Bet You Look Good on the Dance Floor'. I've long suspected the machine has a mind of its own, as it always seems to play the appropriate song. 'Why Does It Always Rain on Me?' when it's pissing down, 'You're Never There' when some girl won't answer her phone.

'Hi, my name's Lucy,' she said.

I paused, trying to think of something smooth, then said, '. . . andandandand . . .' my tongue hanging to my knees. I'd ruined it already. The scene would have to be re-shot.

She blinked in surprise, her heavy lids seeming to take an age to loop down and then up again over her shining eyes. 'Hello?' she said, perhaps wondering if I was mental.

How could I pull this out of the fire? I'd meant to say, 'And what brings a girl like you to a dump like this?' But as the first word left my gaping mouth I realised just how cheesy the line was so I stopped, but then I thought well maybe girls like cheesy, maybe that's where I'd been going wrong, so I started again. Then I froze because I'd taken too long to reply and wasn't sure what to do, I was like a rejected email pinging back and forth between two servers.

'And . . . Dandan . . . Dan. Dan. My name is Dan.' I said. I told you I was clever.

'Dandan? Or just Dan?'

'Sorry, I have a slight speech impediment.'

'Oh, I'm sorry. I'm so rude.'

I waved her concern away.

'Do you know where I could get some coffee?' she asked. 'I'm new here.'

'Sure,' I said, 'I was just going for some myself. It tastes like burned rubber though, I've got to warn you.'

'That's how I like it. It reminds me of my Formula One days.'

'You were in Formula One?' I asked stupidly.

'No that was a joke,' she said, flatly. 'But I don't mind burned coffee, it's like pizza and sex.'

'How's that?' I asked, playing the straight man.

'Even when it's bad, it's good,' she said.

I grinned at her. She was funny as well as beautiful. It wasn't going to happen.

And it didn't happen. But I didn't mind, because even I could see that Lucy and I were more suited to be friends than anything else. We chatted for hours that day. And saw each other regularly thereafter, always at the same table in the rec, always for rubbish coffee.

Lucy gave me two things. She gave me my new name, and she gave me an escape route.

Lucy told me about her life before. She had already lived. She'd been out in the world. She'd travelled, she'd worked, she'd earned money, then blown it all and started again. She was a woman. But she didn't patronise me, she took me at face value, and as an equal. She wasn't like everyone else; she didn't want anything from me. I didn't have to collect her washing, or get a dry tissue for her, or watch Scarlett Johansson films with her. I didn't have to pick up a tin of beans on my way home; I didn't have to tread on eggshells and avoid the subject of absent fathers.

On that first day in the rec, Lucy told me how she came to be there at the Surrey Institute of Art and Design.

She'd worked as a model for a couple of years in London and Paris after being spotted by a scout at a tiny fashion show organised by some of her older sister's friends. She'd only got involved when someone else pulled out. She had to wear an awful shapeless outfit that didn't suit her colouring at all. Nonetheless, the scout saw something in her and arranged an interview for her at an agency in London.

Whilst there, she met Jennifer Jones – 'Jen', already taking the world by storm. She expected to be ignored by the rising star, but found that actually Jen was really, genuinely nice. Lucy had quickly moved on from modelling, getting involved in PR for a fashion company. 'I was going through a difficult time and she made me realise that there was more to life than drink, drugs and boys. That's when I decided to go back to college; I was never going to get a top job as a junior.'

What she said made me think. It made me think I was doing things the wrong way around. How could I study film before I'd studied life itself? What could I make a movie about if I didn't know what the real world was like? Lucy had been there, modelling clothes, then selling them; she knew the industry inside out. She knew the practice; she just needed the theory now.

The more I thought about it, the more running off to London to look for work in the film or TV industry seemed like the answer to all my problems. I'd be away from Mum, away from my whining friends, away from the constant demands of cynical lecturers and bureaucratic college administrators.

Why couldn't I go off and have a whole lifetime before settling down at college again? Why not go to London? Why not earn some dough, get some experience? Meet some women?

So I did.

1

Establishing shot exterior, film/TV studios in London's East End. Wet day. Cut to Dan inside. Pull away and 180 dolly slow tracking sweep to take in cameras, lights etc. surrounding brightly lit stage containing sofa, table, paraphernalia of daytime TV set.

Less than a month later I stood in GTV's studios in London, standing not ten yards away from Jennifer Jones as she was interviewed by Edie Morgan – real-life B-list celebrity and ChannelTalk's great hope. I kept having to pinch myself. One chance meeting and a snap decision one day in the rec, and my life was turned upside down and inside out, spun on its axis and back to front.

OK, so I was only a runner. The pay was lousy and I was living in a rat-infested bedsit in Soho, but I was working, in TV. And I was fifty miles away from Mum, Lidl and the humming clock.

Lucy, brilliant Lucy had arranged the job for me. She was reluctant at first. She argued that I should finish my course, that there was no hurry. But we'd only just started, I couldn't face three years. It was a dull, muggy day at the end of

October, I know because I was trying to remember whether the humming clock was supposed to go forward or back over the coming weekend.

'Spring forward, fall back,' Lucy said, grimacing at the taste of the coffee she'd just swigged. 'That's how you remember.'

'How do you know it's not spring back, fall forward?' I countered.

'It just isn't. Anyway, don't change the subject, you should wait for a bit before you make any hard decisions.'

'You didn't wait before you started your career,' I pointed out.

'And in many ways I regret it,' she replied, reasonably.

'That's not the impression you gave me when you were telling me about the parties, the limos, the fashion shoots in Malaga, or Ibiza.'

'I was just showing off. Why do you think I came back here to study? It can't have been so good if I gave it all up.'

'But you haven't given it up. You've come here to complete your education, the theory side of it. You're going back into that industry.'

'Better to do it the other way round,' she said. 'You're young, you should be here, with your friends. Don't be in such a hurry.'

'Gee, it's really an honour to be patronised by you, Lucy. Thanks.'

She looked at me coolly. She shrugged and said, 'Well, if you're serious I could maybe give you a number, my sister works in TV.'

'Really? That'd be great!' I said, sounding a little too excited, perhaps.

Lucy smiled. 'Her name's Amelie, she works as a researcher for GTV on the morning show. You know it?'

'Of course,' I replied. ChannelTalk was a digital station, but doing well, and bringing in some decent advertising money. It sounded ideal.

I phoned Amelie at the Soho offices where she worked. She was lovely, just like her sister. Apparently they were always looking for runners as they went through them quickly. I asked if it was because they tended to go on to better jobs.

'Umm, sometimes,' she answered.

'Great,' I replied. 'I'm just looking for a foot in the door. I'll work hard.'

'You'll need to,' she said, laughing.

I told Lucy about it, excitedly. 'Amelie seems really nice.'

'She got the looks and the brains,' Lucy complained. 'You'll lose interest in me once you meet Amelie.'

'I'm sure we'll still be friends,' I said, reassuringly. 'After all, I never thought you were that pretty or clever anyway.'

Back in the studio, I thought of Lucy as Jen spoke of her courageous story and her rise to the giddy heights of the fashion world, then her fall from grace. And now, when she had it all, the world swooning at her feet, she was leaving, never to return.

I'd emailed Lucy the night before, when I'd heard that Jen was going to be on the show.

Luce,
Guess who's coming for breakfast – Jennifer Jones!
You a little jealous of my glam life now?
Dan

She replied:

Hi Babe,
Happy for you, Jen is lovely, as I think I may have mentioned before. Say hi to her for me. Not jealous at all, been there, done that. How's the filming going?
Luce

Hi Luce,
No time for filming just now. Too much to learn, too much to see . . .
Dan

GTV has always been focused on the fashion world. The morning chat show is very heavy on clothes and accessories, the audience being mostly teenage girls or stay-at-home mums. The constant stream of young, wannabe models making their way through the building was a real perk of the job for me. Especially when I was asked to look after them, get them drinks, walk them out to the taxi rank, show them to the green room. They mostly ignored me, recognising I was too junior to be worth networking with, but at least they didn't want to be *just friends*. No time-wasters please.

After Jen's interview had finished, she walked off set and chatted to Roland, one of the terrifying floor managers. It's my job to obey people like him without question or hesitation. If Roland asked me to leap from a tall building I think I might just do it, if only to get away from him.

'You,' Roland said, pointing at me. He'd already told me he didn't intend to learn my name; runners never lasted long enough to be worth him spending the time. I was sure that wasn't really true, he just wanted me to prove myself. 'Show Jen to her car please, you know where it is?'

I did, and I said so. Jen smiled at me. 'This way, please.' I said, ducking my head. I felt severely intimidated by her presence. She was beautiful, and so tall. She made Lucy look like a gangly duck. I'd been thinking I might chat to her casually about our mutual acquaintance, but now I was so close, I couldn't have said a word to her, even if it were to say that her hair was on fire.

But she forced the issue as we left the building out the side door and I trotted down the steps feeling awkward, like I'd forgotten how to move my limbs properly.

'What's your name?'

'D-Dan,' I replied, thinking of my first meeting with Lucy. I smiled.

'What's funny?' she asked.

'Oh, just a . . . it seems I have difficulty saying my name when I meet models.'

'How many models do you know?'

'Only one properly, her name's Lucy Hayling. I think you may have met her?'

Jen's face lit up like the Christmas lights on Regent Street. She had that sort of face.

'Of course I know Lucy. She's lovely.'

'She says the same about you.'

'How do you know her?' she asked. I told her about the college, and my decision to run off to London to seek my fortune.

We'd reached her car now, in the restricted parking area, reserved for the VIPs. But she stopped and chatted for a few minutes, and then Jen told me she had to go.

Her driver started the engine and I opened the door for her. She paused before getting in and reached into her bag, pulling out a card and handing it to me. Out of the corner of my eye I saw a taxi drive up and disgorge a passenger as I took the card.

'Thanks,' I said. 'Any advice for a youngster starting out in show biz?'

'Yeah, get out now,' she said. I laughed, but I could see she wasn't entirely joking.

There followed an awkward silence between us. Jen just stood there looking at me with an odd expression. Cars hushed past in the background. A paper cup blew across the car park. I knew just how I'd shoot this scene.

I could almost see it on screen.

She smiled. 'Stay nice, won't you, Dan?' she said, fixing me with an odd gaze. She was otherworldly beautiful. The sign said *Don't Touch.*

I looked back at her, not sure how to respond. 'Err.'

She shook her head. 'I realise you're excited and keen to find your own way. I know you want to make your own mistakes. I won't try to spoil things. Just remember not to expect sympathy or forgiveness. Take what you need from the industry, then get out.' She closed her eyes and took a deep breath.

'Smash and Grab,' she said finally.

'OK,' I said uncertainly. 'Smash and Grab.' This was getting a bit weird.

'Sorry,' she said. 'Just . . . remember what I said. Don't let the industry change you.'

'OK,' I repeated.

Then she did something even weirder, she leaned across, hugged me gently and kissed me on my right cheek. I flushed.

'Please pass on my details to Lucy, won't you?' Jen said. 'Now that I'm settled back in London I'd love to see her again.'

I nodded, unable to speak again as she hit me with the full force of her smile. Then she was gone.

'Now that's a woman,' I said to myself as I turned and trudged back to the studio. The producers liked to have us hanging about at all times, woe betide the runner caught loitering somewhere. I looked up to see the taxi passenger looking at me oddly. It was a young girl, perhaps my age, maybe a little older. She was beautiful, thin, straight-haired with wide eyes. She had the hungry look of an aspiring model about her. Normally I would be all shy and silly when confronted with a girl like this one. But after dealing with Jen, my confidence was sky-high and I wasn't going to go all jelly-legged at the drop of an eyelid.

'Can I help?' I asked in my executive voice.

'Was that Jen Jones?' she asked, incredulous.

'Certainly was,' I replied, showing her the card.

She was star-struck. She started twisting her hair, which is surely something they tell you not to do on your first day of model school.

'What's your name?' I asked.

'Katerina,' she told me, and dropped her eyes shyly.

'Did the agency send you?'

She nodded, not lifting her head. My tummy hatched butterflies.

'Well why don't you come with me?' I said. 'I'll show you where the green room is.'

Grinning evilly, I motioned for her to follow me and stepped confidently across the parking area. This was turning out to be a pretty good day.

Maybe I should jump back a bit and tell you how I got here.

Mum had a mouldy old cousin in London who she never saw. Who she obviously didn't like. Who she made me go and stay with 'until I got myself sorted'. I didn't want to stay with Aunt Mouldy. People running away to the big city to seek adventure weren't supposed to sleep in lavender-encrusted sheets and wake to the sound of porridge on the stove.

'Molly? It's Susan,' Mum had said primly on the phone, the atmosphere already thick as a cheap tortilla.

Molly said something.

'Never mind that,' Mum gritted out, eyes rolling like she was possessed by the demon Nicotinus.

But I didn't have enough cash to spring for a hotel, and I didn't fancy sleeping next to Old Paddy the drunken axeman under Waterloo Bridge, so the day of my big interview I found myself drinking tea in a cat-filled flat in Battersea.

'This place must be worth a bit,' I said to Aunt Mouldy as I sipped, trying to make conversation and choosing a subject I imagined oldies might like to talk about – house prices.

She eyed me suspiciously. Older-looking than Mum, though her junior by a good few years, she was unmarried, and if her attitude to my dear father was representative, unlikely to marry any time soon.

'I really don't know,' she replied. 'I bought it in the seventies so I expect there's been some inflation.'

No need to be so cagey, I didn't say. I'm not going to steal your flat. I'm just making chitchat; I don't give two hoots what your trinket-packed broom-closet is worth.

She disappeared to fill the kettle and I took a quick sweep

around the flat with the camera. The cats watched me with hatred as the humming machine recorded the occasional tables, doilies, *Reader's Digest* magazines and assorted detritus of the unmarried cat-lover.

'I have to go into Soho,' I blurted as she came back. 'I need to meet a friend who's going to give me some tips for the interview.'

She peered at me with a look that suggested I'd just told her I had to dismember one of her Persians. Actually I was just desperate to get out of the stuffy atmosphere. Away from her and the cat hair. It reminded me too much of home, but without any of the comforts. I stumbled as I rushed down the wooden stairs and then out into the thrum and chatter of the big city.

I heart London, I fucking HEART the place. Only someone who's grown up in a provincial town with two buses a day, both going in the wrong direction, can appreciate just how liberating it is to be able to leap on a bus in a matter of minutes and travel wherever you like. I walked across Battersea Bridge first, just to see the river, to smell the urban jungle. And to film my own triumphal arrival like some crusty Roman dude, crossing the Rubik's cube or whatever. Well, there was no one else there to film it. I had my iPod on and playing my guitar anthem playlist, the one I play sparingly because I don't want to use up the magic in the songs.

I kept checking what I'd filmed and redoing it until it was perfect. I was in no hurry.

The great thing about the camera I have is that the quality of the picture is rubbish. Grainy and lacking in vibrancy, it shows a gritty, urban edge to everything, like an artful music video but much cheaper. I jumped on a bus and continued filming from the top floor, enjoying the swaying sensation and secretly hoping it would fall over.

One thing I was missing was a decent computer to download and edit the raw footage I was taking. Mum wouldn't let me take hers, which was crap anyway. I had an idyllic vision that I'd be allowed into the editing site at the TV company at night and I could create my masterpieces there. I wasn't sure it would work that way though. I needed to get the job first, anyway.

As the bus approached Oxford Street, it got stuck in traffic and the driver opened the doors to let us out into the stalled traffic. The pavements were heaving. Foot power was obviously the preferred method of locomotion round here. I joined the throng and was immediately jostled by a skinhead with a dog on a string. Feeling like a hick I grabbed my wallet pocket. He mistook the gesture as a threat and turned, bristling as much as his rabid-looking dog. 'Sorry,' I said, not wanting to touch this guy, let alone get into a fight. He had scabs on his knuckles.

'You will be,' he snarled and moved off. I shivered and wished I'd had the camera rolling.

I shrugged it off and moved into the depths of Soho, looking for St Anne's Court and the door to number twenty.

* * *

The Court wasn't what I'd expected. It was more of an alley if I'm honest. Urine-soaked. Litter-strewn. Very edgy and that, guv, but a little unpleasant, truth be told. The door, however, was just what I'd expected. Gold chrome, touchpad security system, CCTV. The building looked like the back of someone else's building, and probably was. 'GTV' said a tiny plate next to the top buzzer. My interview wasn't for another half-hour. I pulled out the camera and filmed the door. A homeless guy lay watching me across the alley. I caught his reflection in the chrome panel of the door and hit record.

Then the door swung open and I found myself filming a nice pair of lightly tanned legs. I stood quickly.

'Hello,' said the girl who owned the legs, 'can I help you?' She was attractive in a slightly older-than-her-years way. I wondered if she liked cats.

Caught on the horns. Should I run for it? Or did this girl work for GTV? Mustn't take chances. I stepped up. 'Hi, I'm Dan Lewis, I'm here for an interview . . . at GTV. Err, do you work there?'

'I do,' she smiled. 'I'm Amelie.'

'Great!' I said too loudly, and then I saw the resemblance to Lucy. They were similar, but Amelie didn't carry herself in the same way, she was too . . . normal (psst, plumper).

'I'm early,' I said, then without thinking, 'I wasn't looking at your legs.'

'OK,' she said, bemused or annoyed, I couldn't tell. 'I'm popping out for lunch, do you want to come and have a quick coffee? I can give you some tips.'

'Terrific!' I said. 'I'd like that.' Without meaning to, I'd said it in a way that implied I thought she was asking me out on a date. Which of course she wasn't.

In a greasy spoon round the corner I was pleased to see she ordered chicken, chips, peas and gravy. With a diet Coke cos that would make all the difference. I ordered a coffee because that's what she'd said I should have. We made small talk until her food arrived. I couldn't help but notice there was a slight bruise on her left temple. She looked up and I dropped my eyes to her food and pretended to be fascinated.

She saw me eyeing her plate and she did that middle-class scrunchy face thing.

'Hangover,' she said, 'Scotch and dry,' explaining it all.

'Non-stop parties I suppose, in this business,' I replied hopefully.

'If you can get yourself invited to the ones with a free bar, yes,' she said. 'Otherwise you can't afford the dry, let alone the Scotch.'

I found her easy to talk to, as I had with Lucy. Though there was something else there too. DE-fence.

'Who's interviewing you?' she asked, cramming a forkful of barn-reared chicken into her Hampshire-reared mouth.

I peered at the email I'd printed out. 'Elena Jotavich,' I said.

'She's John Waters' assistant,' Amelie replied, stuffing more food in. 'John will probably interview you, though it won't last long.'

‘Why’s that?’ I said, worried.

‘He’s a first impressions guy.’ Chew chew.

I raised an eyebrow.

She swallowed. ‘He thinks he can sum people up in a couple of minutes, tell whether they’re winners or losers. You’ll either get the job straight away, or he’ll tell you to get the hell out of the building.’ She turned her attention back to her plate.

‘Shit, I’ve gotta go,’ I said, realising what the time was. The chat hadn’t made me less nervous. I didn’t relish the thought of turning up back at home with no job and eight months to go before term started again.

John Waters kept me waiting for twenty-four minutes. I could see him in his glass-doored office through a gap in the blinds. He was a bustler, a fusstler. He didn’t seem to be doing much.

Elena was horrible. The receptionist, a pretty blonde, had told me to go through and introduce myself to her. She was a middle-aged lady, sharp-featured and disapproving. She had one of those fringes like the paint-ad dogs.

‘Hello,’ I said, palms sweating a bit. ‘I’m Dan Lewis, here to see Mr Waters.’

She peered at me disdainfully, and then sneered. She actually sneered.

‘Do you have any experience in TV?’ she asked in a tone that suggested she knew damn well I didn’t. Who’s doing the interview here?

'No, but I'm a hard worker.'

'You don't know the meaning of hard work,' she said and waved me to a chair outside Waters' office. I sat. She reached into a large bag of marshmallows and popped one in her thin-lipped mouth. I could see her computer screen. She was playing solitaire.

After keeping me waiting Waters stared at me in silence for three more minutes as I fidgeted on his enormous and enormously comfortable sofa. He'd called me into his office and waved a hand vaguely towards the furniture as I followed him in. 'Take a seat,' he'd said. I thought he'd waved towards the sofa so I sat there, then realised he'd meant for me to sit at the chair at his desk. It was too late to change now though so I sat as straight as I could so I wouldn't be too disadvantaged by the height difference.

'Mind if I take a photo?' he barked.

I was too surprised to say no. Did he think I was applying for a presenter's job? He could surely see I wasn't a model.

'For your *application*,' he said, seeing my confusion. He held up a tiny gadget and clicked a photo of me doing a goldfish impression. He peered at it. Snorted and didn't take another. He glanced at my CV. Despite my discomfort, I couldn't help but notice again how nice the sofa was. It must have cost a bomb. One day, I'd have an office with an uber-sofa just like this one, except bigger. Uberer.

'For fuck's sake, why do you want to work *here*, Dan?' he snapped malevolently, as if I'd gone for a job in an Al-Qaeda cell.

I was ready for this. 'I love film, I love TV. I want to be a film-maker, so I need . . .' but that was it. He'd heard enough.

He made a buzzing-farting noise. 'Not looking for a film-maker. Job description says Runner,' he said, pointing triumphantly at the piece of paper in front of him.

'We . . . Well I can do that, I realise I have to start at the bottom . . .'

'Fuck me but you didn't, did you? You started blathering about being a film-maker. You're already thinking of the top. Do that somewhere else, no place for ambition here. I need someone who'll get me cup of coffee . . .' and he leaned across the cluttered desk and loomed over me and the mega-sofa, 'and fucking LOVE doing it. For EVER.'

And that was it. That was the interview. He'd summed up me and my eighteen years of uncomplainingly getting coffee for self-important people in less than five minutes and I could already hear Aunt Mouldy saying, 'Never mind, I'll put the kettle on. Here, hold this cat.' I could already smell Mum's fags and sense the tension in the air back home.

He made to stand up and I saw the hand come towards me to cut off my windpipe, or maybe just my future, when someone coming into the office behind me interrupted us. Waters hadn't bothered to close the door behind him, I was *that* important.

'What do you want?' Waters snapped irritably and I turned involuntarily. It was Amelie.

'I just wanted to let you know I have that video you were

looking for,' she said. Then 'Who's this?' she asked, turning to me. I stared back at her. Had she gone mad? We'd just had lunch together.

Waters, meanwhile, had gone quite white at the mention of the video. 'He's here for an interview,' he said absently, his mind on something else. 'We'd just finished.' He obviously wanted to get rid of me so he could discuss this mysterious video. 'Hadn't we, um-Dan?'

'Umm, yes, yes we had,' I said, refusing to look at Amelie any more. I felt my face flushing with the awfulness of it all. I just wanted to get the hell out of there. More running away. This would have to stop at some point.

'Well I hope you've given him the job,' Amelie said, smartly. I swivelled to look at her. She winked.

Waters was sideswiped. He patently hadn't given me the job. He said nothing, just stared at the girl, open-mouthed.

'He has a good face,' she said. 'I think he's someone who can be trusted with important . . . things,' she said, smiling sweetly at Waters. She went on, 'I'm a very good judge of character.'

Waters thought for a long time, just standing there looking back and forth between us. Then he asked me when I could start. Amelie plonked a video cassette down on his desk and disappeared. Something had just happened there. Amelie had got me the job, but how? And why? What was on the video? Even before I'd started, intrigue surrounded me.

I left GTV's offices with an evil grin plastered on my mug,

Waters' eyes burning a hole between my shoulders. I also had two pieces of paper; one was a confirmation of job offer, and the other was Amelie's phone number. I'd spoken to her on the way out and she'd told me coolly she was delighted I'd be working there, as though the whole episode with the video hadn't happened. What a cool place to work this was going to be. Secret spy stuff going on all over the place.

Amelie suddenly seemed much younger than I'd thought before, as she stood playing with her hair while I scribbled down the numbers she was reading out. She told me she had a place in Hackney, which was cheaper, but no cleaner than Soho. Which was where I was intending to live. How cool is that?

I plugged my iPod earpieces in and hit shuffle. My sentient iPod thumped into Blur's 'Song 2' and I raised my fists in triumph as I stormed down the narrow pavement.

I'd arrived.

2

Soundtrack plays grungy urban music. Shoulder camera with fish-eye lens travels north up Wardour Street from Shaftesbury Avenue. Assorted extras pass by. Homeless man begging with dog. Businessmen, tourists, stylish women, yobs, drunks etc. Slo-mo fast-mo. Camera turns to watch elegant woman pass. She turns her head and winks.

It was pretty obvious I couldn't stay with Aunt Mouldy for long, and as soon as I knew the job was mine I started looking. It would have been cheaper of course to stay with her, but she didn't like me, the cats hated me and I wasn't in love with them either. Besides, I had a funky job in Soho. I was urban-hip, trip-hop, pretty fly for a white guy. I couldn't live in a house with Werther's Originals wrappers in the potpourri. I hadn't been confident I'd find anywhere in central London. Even though my needs weren't great.

Amelie pointed me in the direction of a low-life estate agent up three flights of stairs in an office overlooking Berwick Street market. The clientele weren't much to look at. Thin grizzled crusties and fat ladies with too many handbags. On the other hand, I thought as I took a number and waited to be called by the cheap-suited, Alan Sugar-wannabe behind the one crappy old desk, if people like this can afford to live in Soho, then so can I.

I'd been looking around in the last few days; it might seem that all the buildings in Soho are just shops, but above them are flats, where people live, you can see them hanging out the windows smoking fags and yelling at each other. These people weren't yuppies either; some of them were pretty chavvie to be honest. Maybe Soho was just so grotty no one with money wanted to live here. Suited me. I just wanted somewhere close to work. Close to here, where things were happening. I'd already witnessed three fights and an arrest. I was starting to get to know the homeless guys who wandered up and down the maze of ancient streets here.

Now, once I'd found out how much I was getting paid, £10,500 a year, I sat down at Aunt Mouldy's writing 'bureau' as she called it and did some rapid calculations. I deliberately chose the back of an envelope for the purpose.

Back then I had no idea what stuff cost but I made some guesses and came up with this:

Salary per month – £875
Food: £100
Booze: £210 (show your working: average 2 pints @ £3.50 per pint a night x 30 nights = £210)
Savings: £100

Electricity/Gas: £30
Going out: £100
Total: £540

Leaving £335 for rent. Surely I could find something for £335?

The agent smirked when I told him how much I could afford and gave me three addresses to check out. The first was described as a flat share, but there was only one bathroom for eight residents and three of the beds were in the living room. The vacant room had no window and stank of someone's cheesy feet. It smelled so bad that I was convinced the cheesy feet's owner must have accidentally left them there under the bed. I didn't have the guts to check.

The second place seemed all right at first. It was described as a studio/bedsit. In a basement in a grotty building just behind a theatre. I was impressed at first till I realised that I'd be sharing it with another guy who'd already bagsied the bedroom and was paying nearly double what I was. I'd be allocated a pull-down bed in an area which was described as a box room, but which looked suspiciously like an alcove in the hallway. I also noticed the other guy's CD collection. He had James Blunt.

The third place was the worst. There was someone next door who I think had put his speakers facing the wall and was playing that spine-grinding thrash metal where it sounds like three guitarists are trying to make their guitars sound like drums. Duh-du-du-duh, du-du-du-du-duh. There was a grimy window that let in no light, making the place look like the basement Jodie Foster staggers around blindly in at the end of *Silence of the Lambs*. I didn't bother looking at the bathroom, convinced it would be filled with giant moths.

So I tramped back to the estate agents and revised my calculations. I'd just have to drink less. Or, eat less. Or, let's be really full of honesty here, save less.

'What can I get for £450?' I asked Sir Alan. He raised what looked like a plucked eyebrow and scribbled an address.

I was so relieved it wasn't like the others I gave the landlord the deposit straight away using the last of the money I'd been saving from my Saturday job. His name was Ronnie and he looked a dodgy geezer, with greasy hair and gaps in his teeth, which seemed to change position each time he closed his mouth. Which wasn't often. 'There you go, Maestro,' he said, handing me the keys.

It was a tiny but neat and nearly odourless room in a loft-space bedsit overlooking Wardour Street, a 35mm film canister's throw from work. The bathroom was shared, but there were only two other rooms with mine on the top floor. The bathroom downstairs got heavier traffic, used as it was by a dozen drunks sharing the five cheaper rooms down there. By the smell of them most of them pissed in their clothes anyway. The landlord said they never came up here, having difficulty with the narrow stairs.

The best thing about it was that it had a tiny window with a view down Wardour Street towards Shaftesbury Avenue. A hundred yards away was the gabled roof of the Shaftesbury theatre. I soon discovered I could, with difficulty, squeeze out of the little window and sit quite comfortably in a well behind a lintel, or parapet or whatever it's called. It wasn't much of a roof terrace, but no one could see me out here. I closed my eyes and soaked up the vaguely menacing hum of London's red-light district down below. After unpacking, the first thing I did was whip out the camera and take a few artful, moody shots, trying to bring out the grungy, Boho feeling I got from the place. I ran out of tape and replaced it with my last blank. I really needed a computer to get this footage edited. I pinned up my *Midnight Express* poster and felt like I'd arrived.

Food I got from a Europa a few shops down the street. This sort of convenience would have helped back in Keenham when Mum remembered something else she'd forgotten to ask me to get last time I went to the shops. There was only a tiny fridge, a sink and a microwave in the bedsit but I'd managed to blag a toaster from the Mouldster so I bought a loaf of bread and some butter and Marmite. And four cans of the cheapest lager they had.

It was only when I got back to the flat I remembered I had no TV; I hate sitting in silence. The iPod was going to get a lot of abuse. I hit shuffle and the clever little bugger played Gorillaz' 'All Alone'.

Hi Luce,
Got the job, here's a piccie of me on my Soho roof terrace,
Love
Dan

Hi Babes
That's great, in a way, and not in another,
Luce

Don't start that again

Sorry. I'm pleased for you. You've made the decision now so I'm behind you sweetie.

Cheers, hey, Amelie's much prettier than you.

Knew you'd fancy her! She is gorgeous.

Didn't say I fancied her, or that she's gorgeous, she's just much prettier than you.

Hate you.

Night.

Night. Don't really hate you. Miss you.

Miss you too.

'What the *fuck* is this?' Waters choked off, turning a worrying colour. It was like one of those animals you study in biology that demonstrates agitation by changing colour. And swearing a lot.

'Err, it's your post,' I said carefully, wondering if I were walking into a trap. Waters' assistant, Elena, was away, and one of my many duties was to do her job when she was away, which seemed to be quite a lot. Getting Waters his post was one of her jobs.

'Un-opened! You brainless gimp. Do you think someone in my position opens his own post?'

'Of course not,' I replied smoothly, having learned that it didn't really matter what you said to Waters, you just had to say it calmly and in a tone that suggested you had everything under control.

I'd been at GTV three weeks or so and on the whole was enjoying myself. Waters was a nightmare and the first couple of times he'd screamed at me I thought I was in serious trouble, but he tended to forget about things immediately and you were fine until the next time you put a stapler down too loudly, or couldn't find a file immediately. I never had time to file anything so spent a large chunk of my day scrabbling through my filing tray. Not that I had my own filing tray – I shared a desk (no computer) with the other two runners. Though a lot of the time I was sat at Elena's desk outside Waters' office, trying to figure out how the phones worked.

I also spent quite a bit of time at the East End studio, helping out with tedious jobs no one else wanted to do. Making tea, mostly. Buying small items from local shops. Very occasionally I got to go out on location with one of the film units; I loved that the most, even though everyone shouted at me and made me do mind-destroying things like pick up litter and get blankets for cold talent.

The Soho office held about forty people and was split into two sections joined by a narrow corridor. The front office held Reception, the showrooms, meeting rooms, the offices of important people and a dozen or so support staff in an open-plan section in the middle. The back section was where the techno-geeks and IT people sat. We called it the gulag. There was no natural light and the aircon hummed like a thousand Lidl clocks.

Most of my job involved sitting around for ages being ready to do stuff, then jumping to obey an order, cocking it up and getting yelled at. There were two other runners, James and Rashid, who had perfected the art of being slightly further away from the person who wanted stuff done than I was. I spent a lot of time trotting around Soho (running, I suppose) buying arcane items, dropping things off and picking things up. I had to do the post run twice a day and deliver piles of documents or sales material around the building. I had no idea how anything worked and I wasn't allowed to ask. I was expected to just follow orders to the letter and run while I was doing it.

I'd discovered one or two things about the company from Amelie, who was the only person who'd talk to me (as opposed to shout at me) apart from James and Rashid. The flagship show, filmed at the rented studios in East London, was *The Morning Show*. In theory it was a current affairs programme but in reality it was just a fashion programme with a couple of token 'news' stories about Jade Goody's latest fashion howler or live reports of some glittering award ceremony. It was a scam basically. Designers paid a premium to have their clothes featured on the show, adding considerably to the advertising revenue a show could normally expect in that slot. They used new young models desperate for a break and paid them nothing. Part of Amelie's job was to first find them and then dump them when they started asking for more money.

I told James about the bollocking I'd got from Waters and he told me not to worry about it. We were standing on the fire escape at the back of the building. James and Rashid popped out two or three times an hour sometimes, smoking endless fags and flicking ash with quick, nervous motions over the side. There was no policy against smoking out there. I don't know why they were so surreptitious about it. As long as there was one of us around at all times, we could do pretty much what we liked. They'd given up offering me fags. I was determined not to start. Mum had set me a good example that way.

'Don't worry about Waters,' James said. 'He's an arse.'

‘And a gym fraud, I’ve been told,’ Rashid added. ‘Melody goes to the same gym and she’s seen him there.’

I crinkled my forehead. ‘What’s a gym fraud?’

‘You know, all gong and no dinner. Got all the gear and goes regularly but just farts about stretching and chatting most of the time,’ James said.

‘Yeah,’ added Rashid. ‘And when he’s finished on a machine, he waits till he thinks no one’s looking and changes the weight on to the heaviest setting to try and impress the next person.’

‘What a knob!’ I said. ‘I had noticed that he’s not got a six-pack so much as a keg.’

‘Anyway, you’ll feel better after you’ve had a couple of drinks tonight,’ Rashid said.

I shook my head. ‘Thanks, guys, I’d love to but I’m skint until next week, I still haven’t had my first pay cheque.’

James grinned. ‘You won’t need money, you just need to be prepared to bullshit,’ he said in his drawling Australian accent.

‘What’s that?’ I said, wishing I wasn’t the new kid.

‘We’ve got some extra invites to a free bar bash at Soho House.’

I had no idea what Soho House was, but I wanted to be there, drinking free drinks.

‘Great! One for me?’

‘Yeah no probs,’ Rashid said.

‘What’s it for?’ I asked, naively.

'Eh?' James said, cocking his head.

'What's the party for, what's the celebration?'

They looked at each other, and laughed.

'Free food and grog, mate, that's the celebration.'

Elena was horrible. Did I mention that already? She'd pass on work to me, supposedly from Waters, or one of the other producers, but which was so obviously her work. Like her filing, or making cups of tea for Waters' guests, or answering her phone while she went to a three-hour lunch. Then she'd come back smelling of booze and making snide comments about my haircut.

I don't know why she hated me. Maybe she didn't. She was pretty nasty to everyone. Once she spied plump Melody wearing a floral dress and said, 'Oh sorry, Melody, didn't see you there, you seem to be disguised as an armchair.'

I avoided her sneery gaze as I swept towards the post table at the front of the office.

'Coffee!' Waters yelled as I passed. I fought back the urge to say, 'Not for me, thanks!' and waved in acknowledgement. He'd already gone back into his office. Waters' coffee came from outside. There was a perfectly good cafetière in the kitchen AND one of those poncy machines that actually make pretty good cappuccinos (cappuccini?) but he insisted I go to Starbucks for his. He also demanded I get the non-Fairtrade one. He was the sort of guy who drives an SUV in the city just to annoy environmentalists. He was always going on about conspiracies by the politically-correct brigade. I just smiled. James and Rashid called him Jeremy Clarkson.

I headed for the door just as Amelie was showing someone out. She turned.

My stomach sucked itself in automatically as I realised it was Katerina. My Model.

'Hi there,' I said, feeling full of myself and fully capable of carrying on where I'd left off the first time we'd met. She smiled. She remembered me. Amelie rolled her eyes and left me to it.

'How'd it go?' I asked, wishing I'd brought an executive-style case or something to make me look more important. A filofax maybe.

She shrugged. 'OK, I suppose. I think they're looking for older girls at the moment. My agent said not to get too hopeful.'

'Who's your agent?' I asked

'Marj Newman.'

I nodded as if I'd heard good things about her.

'She knows her stuff,' I said, convincingly. I held the door open and we stepped out into the chilly February air, dank with condensed traffic fumes.

Katerina looked at me, concerned. 'So you're telling me I'm too young for Paris?'

Whatever, dude, I wanted to say. No idea what you're talking about.

Instead: 'I don't think so, but what do I know? I'm just a . . .'

She fixed me with a calculating look; she wanted this information. What am I? Another crunch time. Crunchy town, London.

'. . . assistant producer. I know nothing about modelling.'

She seemed unsure. I'd used the title Assistant Producer as I'd noticed there were tons of them, some very young and with pretty low-flying, bottom-feeding jobs to do. It also sounded as though I was there, on the very cusp of power.

'Though I think you look pretty good in that!' I said with a James Bond smile. Corny is good, but don't overdo it, I told myself.

But she smiled.

'I wonder if . . .' she began and touched her hair. My ears pricked, and there was other movement.

'Yes?' I said glancing up the street as if to say I needed to get on but I couldn't quite drag myself away from this girl.

'You know Jane Macauley, don't you?'

Jane Macauley was our 'resident' fashion designer. She had a mutually beneficial relationship with *The Morning Show*. She gave us style. We gave her publicity.

Oh, so she wasn't asking me out. Of course she wasn't asking me out.

'I've been trying to get an interview at her label.'

I blinked. I suppose agency loyalty wasn't a huge issue for out-of-work models.

I smiled. 'You want me to put in a word for you?'

She nodded shyly. And stroked her hair again. Was she playing me? Well maybe that could work two ways. 'Why don't you come to Soho House tonight? I'll put you on the guest list. Macauley should be there.' Her eyes widened. 'Give me your number,' I said briskly. She rummaged in her tiny bag and handed me a card.

I wasn't lying. Macauley probably would be there.

'And will you be there?'

'Wouldn't miss it for the world.'

'Great,' she said. 'I'll need someone to look after me.' She dropped her eyes primly, playing the little girl. I swallowed and stepped away.

'Gotta go, see you tonight,' I walked ten feet and turned around briefly. She was still watching me. What had just happened there? I felt exhilarated, and a bit frightened. As though I'd just been offered some coke. I smiled and turned back, narrowly avoiding walking into a lamppost. I went to the chippy and had a coffee, my hands shaking as I fumbled for the change.

I fucking heart London.

When I got back to the office I asked Rashid to put Katerina's name on the guest list and winked when he gave me an enquiring look. Back at my desk Waters swung by, in surprisingly sunny mood, apparently.

'Good lunch?' he asked. He still didn't know my name.

'Thanks, yeah,' I replied, a little taken aback. 'I went to the Plaice to Eat.'

He nodded and smiled. 'I know it well. Great mushy peas.'

'The best!' I agreed, feeling like a prat. He stood and moved off, then stopped and turned.

'Oh, one more thing . . .'

'Yep?'

'Where's my *sodding* coffee, you little *arse*?'

Some women openly size up other women by casting a sneering look down to their painful shoes and back up again. Imagine a room full of women like that, all sneering at each other. Sneering at the clothes everyone else was wearing, though they all looked pretty much alike to me. That was what the party was like.

'Look at them,' Amelie spat. Sneering a bit herself. 'Look at how they treat each other. Judging!'

I nodded. Surprised by her venom. She'd had a couple of drinks already.

'If you don't like what women are wearing this season, ladies,' she went on, 'I suggest you do something about it, you are the leading lights of the fashion industry after all.'

That's what the party was like. A hundred or so people clustered around an empty catwalk in a too-small room full of plush. Sneaking glances at each other. Contemptuous of what they saw. Amelie spotted Waters and went over to chat to him about something. I went off to the bar. Everyone ignored me. Especially my colleagues. Rashid, James and Amelie were the only people approximately on my level. There were the guys who worked in the back office of course, the technical guys. But they were so geeky that no one told them about parties like this. If asked, James would give them the wrong date, and venue.

'Where's my *sodding* pint, you little *arse*?' Rashid chortled as I handed him a bottle of Becks. Everyone had heard Waters having a go at me over the coffee lapse, as he'd intended.

I scowled at him. 'This is all they had.'

'Pints aren't in this year,' James added, 'people are drinking apple schnapps with Evian these days.'

'Schnapps is the new black,' Rashid said.

'I've never had schnapps,' I ventured, somewhat unwisely. The boys looked at each other like Ant and Dec do when they're about to make someone eat testicles.

Amelie wandered back to join us, swigging another drink, and she bumped into me; I felt her right breast brush against my chest. She swayed back, whoopsing, and grabbed my arm for support. I instinctively flexed the bicep and tried to hold it taut. James was watching the performance with interest.

'Sorry,' Amelie said, and let go of my arm. 'Remind me who invited you boys again?'

'We're here on business,' Rashid said earnestly.

'Oh yes?' Amelie replied. 'What business exactly?'

'The business of scoring free stuff,' Rashid responded, bowing slightly. I laughed.

Elena stalked past, glass in hand, and fixed us with a baleful glare. 'Enjoying your free drinks?'

Rashid held up his bottle, grinning. 'Thanks, yes.'

The battle-axe scowled and moved on.

James looked at me. 'If you don't grab free stuff when you can in this job, you starve, or go mad.'

'It's one of the perks,' Amelie agreed. 'None of us get paid much, and until you shin a little way up the greasy pole none of us has a very enjoyable job either, so this sort of thing is part of the reward. It all gets charged to some client somewhere; no one really minds as long as you keep your nose clean.'

The others nodded. 'We joke about it,' James said, 'but seriously, make sure you grab loads of stuff, everyone else does it. All the way up.' And as if to illustrate his point, I caught sight of Waters on the other side of the room, laughing like a hyena's drain and helping himself to two glasses of champagne, one of which he up-ended and poured down his pock-marked throat immediately. The other he held on to for the look of the thing.

A voluptuous girl with a permanent grin wandered over to join us.

'Amelie!' she cried.

'Lois! Sweetheart,' Amelie replied and hugged her friend before turning to introduce her to me.

'Dan, this is my bestie mate, Lois. She works for Web Mode.'

'Hello,' I said, not knowing who Web Mode were. I later found out they were the most influential web-based fashion channel on the planet. They were people worth knowing in the fashion world, the Web being so much more immediate than the glossies, newspapers or even TV. People turned to them for the most up-to-the-minute news.

Amelie brushed my arm again and I wondered what was going on there. I wasn't particularly interested in Amelie; she was pretty, and more sexual than Lucy, and she seemed to be giving me messages, but there was Katerina in the wings. I didn't want to get tied down with anything serious just now, when London and the job seemed to be offering so much. But on the other hand, it had been a long, looong time for me, and maybe Amelie was just looking for something casual anyway.

Either way, no point burning bridges until you have to. Beggars can't be choosers. Don't look a gift horse in the mouth and so on. I shifted slightly so that my hand touched her hip. She didn't move away. Lois watched us carefully.

'Dan!'

It was Katerina. I moved quickly away from Amelie and waved.

'Excuse me,' I said to the others, avoiding Amelie's look, and walked to meet the model. I certainly didn't want the others screwing things up either by accident or, more likely, on purpose.

'Great you could come,' I said smoothly, slipping into producer mode.

'You look nice,' she said.

'Thanks, I was going to say that.'

'This old thing?' she said, grinning. She had great

lips. Wonderful teeth. Fragile-looking cheekbones tempered by the softest skin I've seen on anyone over the age of six. She was so beautiful I hadn't really noticed what she was wearing. I looked now. It was pretty much the same sort of thing all the other women were wearing in the room. Except Amelie.

'Is Jane Macauley here?' she asked.

I had no idea.

'I saw her earlier,' I said. Not a lie. Macauley had been in the office today and I'd seen her then. Though the way I said it suggested that I might have seen her to talk to her, rather than just seen the back of her head in the meeting room.

'Let me get you a drink,' I said.

I got her a few drinks as it happened, though I'm not sure she drank any of them. They just seemed to disappear, glass and all. I struggled a bit at first. She was pretty rather than clever and she just kept asking me loads of questions about Macauley, Jen, *The Morning Show* and the forthcoming fashion week in Paris, which apparently we were supposed to be covering for TV. I blustered as well as I could but she was getting a little frustrated I think, until Melody passed by and I grabbed her and set her off. Melody is a mumsy fashion editor on the show and one of those people who you ask a question of and they just talk at you about it ceaselessly until you walk away or hit them with a shovel.

I took the opportunity and popped to the unisex loo. There were a lot of people there, men and women, all hanging around the sinks, some bent over. They turned and looked at me suspiciously before turning back to whatever they were doing.

Waters was there, and a couple of the other directors.

I decided I didn't really want to know. But in the cubicle, I remembered what Mr Blake, my film tutor, had told me, that a cameraman should always be looking for the money shot, even if it seems like an invasion of privacy or in bad taste. That if in doubt, one should take the shot and consider the morality later, preferably after you've banked the cheque. I flipped open the camcorder and held it under my armpit, a trick I'd perfected back at college when I was trying to get some footage of the Dean when he was thought by the student mag to be fiddling the books. He wasn't, as it turned out, but he was shagging his secretary. That story got spiked.

As did the secretary, come to think of it.

I left the cubicle and walked smoothly over to the door, then swivelled as I opened it, the viewfinder pointed straight at the assembled dignitaries. Waters was wiping his nose and sniffing; Jane Macauley, the designer, was hoovering up a line as fat and white as a piece of chalk.

I left the loo and packed the camcorder away. I had no idea what interest anyone might have in this film, but it wasn't going to hurt, and when I came to make a video diary I could pixellate the faces so as not to cause any trouble.

I decided against going straight back to Katerina, knowing that Melody would be able to answer all Katerina's questions, keep her occupied and give me a break so I could go and talk to James and Rashid for a bit. And as I was ninety per cent sure that Melody didn't really know who I was or what my job title was, I didn't think she'd give my little fib away. Amelie had disappeared.

'What's your secret?' James asked, smiling at me in a manner that suggested he believed it impossible that any woman could find me attractive.

'I guess some guys just have it, and some don't,' I replied, not wanting to get too deeply into the subject.

Rashid was a bit pissed by now. He descended into a giggling fit.

'I think you made the wrong move, mate, Amelie was up for it tonight,' James said.

I bristled. 'Don't talk like that about her, eh?' I said, trying not to sound belligerent.

'It's true, mate,' said James. 'Amelie's always up for a bit of bump and grind, or so the rumours have it.'

I said nothing, unsure of myself.

'Apparently she did Waters in his office the week she started,' Rashid went on, glugging his Becks. The party was going full steam now and someone had pumped up the music. Some horrendous world music jazz-funk mass of shite.

It was as uncomfortable listening to the heads-up on Amelie as it was listening to the music, but I wanted to know. Had I just had a lucky escape?

'She can't be up to much in the sack though cos she's

been stuck as an assistant researcher for two years now,' James added, chortling at his own observation.

'Maybe she gave him the clap,' Rashid suggested, thoughtfully.

I'd heard enough. I went back to Katerina and rescued her from Melody, who seemed to have sated her enormous appetite for information.

'Macauley's gone,' I said, hazy with lost respect and too much bottle-foamy beer. 'There's no one important here, sorry.'

She tutted and looked around as though I was bullshitting. Which I was.

'Wanna go and get a drink somewhere quieter?' I said. I was tired and wanted to crack this wide open. If she was interested in me, she'd come. If it was just contacts she wanted, she'd probably hang around.

'Sure,' she said.

As we left together we passed Amelie, looking the worse for wear and stumbling a little as she came out of the loos. Lois was there, supporting her. I smiled wanly.

'Seeya,' she said, and turned away.

3

Aerial shot from helicopter over London. Camera swoops and dives between buildings. Fast-mo fix on Dan. Rapid zoom on to his face. Close-up wide-angle. He grins.

'I know a good pub,' I said hopefully, scanning the road, trying to remember if we were on Dean or Greek Street.

'I don't really like pubs,' she said. 'There's a nice bar on Old Compton Street.' I grimaced. I couldn't afford a bar. Oh well, it was payday in a few days, I'd just have to use my overdraft, this was an emergency.

She led me to a place called Baa. With a sheep theme. Crowds of muscular men thronged, or possibly thonged, around the bar. The barmen wore Little-Bo-Peep hats or shearers' overalls if their torsos were buff enough. The music was jaw-achingly loud. Why did she think this was the best place to come? Is it because she worried we might have nothing to talk about? So we should therefore go somewhere we wouldn't be able to hear each other? She was probably right.

'Dry white wine,' she said, without enthusiasm.

Fine, well I wasn't totally enthused about jostling for position with the sweat-squad for twenty minutes whilst waiting to order over-priced drinks, but there was nothing else to do. I left her by a sticky wall-table, reasonably sure none of the guys in this place would try to pick her up.

I had an idea to buy a bottle of wine and take it back with two glasses. She might be inclined to drink more with a bottle available. Though what then? I could hardly take her back to my place; she thought I was a producer. Oh well, cross that bridge when we come to it. Actually, the fact that we didn't have anywhere to go increased the chances she might actually want to come back somewhere, in the same way you're more likely to score if you're wearing your grossest pair of pants or haven't washed your sheets for two months. In the back of my head I was dimly aware that there was no way this was going to happen. Things like this didn't happen to people like me. Or at least not to me specifically.

I took an age to get to the bar, then another age to attract the attention of one of the Bo-Peeps. As I waited, I whipped the camera out of my satchel and took a quick sweep around the bar before zooming in on my date, leaning winsomely against a pillar. She was tall. But I was no short-arse. She didn't tower over me.

'Can I help you?' I jumped and asked for a bottle of white wine. The barman gave me a funny look.

'No white wine, we've got champagne.'

'No white wine?' What kind of bar was this?

He shrugged. He could tell I was straight, I knew it. He held me in contempt. He might even be thinking about IDing me.

'Champagne,' I said.

'Wow!' she said when I returned from my adventure. 'I only wanted a glass.'

I waved it away. 'I didn't want to have to go back again.' I poured the drinks. I hadn't looked at the receipt, just punched my number in. Free money. Plenty of time to pay later. Roll on payday. I couldn't keep doing this sort of thing. Let's hope the Katerina thing was resolved one way or the other quickly.

'So,' she asked, 'are you going to Paris?'

This again? 'I might do, I haven't decided yet. There are some people I'd like to catch up with.'

She nodded, smiling.

'And others I don't want to catch up with me.'

She laughed. This was going well. I topped up her glass.

'So how long have you been a model?'

'A while. I've only really done catalogues so far, nothing on TV or in the glossies.'

'A matter of time, I'm sure. You just need your foot in the door,' I said vaguely.

She nodded again, staring hard at me.

'Thanks for asking me . . . along, tonight,' she said, her eyes sliding down.

'Thanks for coming.'

We chatted for a while, filling the airtime, just. There

were no fireworks, but it wasn't horrible. Not for me anyway. I couldn't tell with her. Couldn't tell what she was thinking.

'Oh hell, my last train leaves soon,' she said after twenty minutes of controlled small talk. 'I have to go.'

We'd hardly started the champagne. I stood with my mouth open, wanting to offer her the use of my bed, but realising just how many reasons there were this was a bad idea. She caught my intention though and gave me a finger-wagging smile.

'I'll walk you to the station,' I said, thinking about the half-bottle of champagne I hadn't yet paid for.

It was a relief to get out of the sheep-pen and walk through the cool air, down crispy duck-scented Gerrard Street. She lived in New Cross, a place I'd never heard of, and her train left from Charing Cross. We chatted quietly as we walked, my head clearing. She was a nice girl. Though it was possible she was bit dim. I told myself she was just young. She didn't know who Almodovar was, or Fellini. But she'd heard of Steven Soderbergh.

For my part I had to admit I wasn't familiar with Stella McCartney's new range, or anything about the Italian Wunderkinder. 'What sort of programmes do you produce?' she asked, puzzled once I'd convincingly demonstrated my ignorance of La Mode.

'Oh fashion,' I said, 'but I'm involved in the production-ey side rather than the fashion-ey side.'

She seemed to accept this.

God I was good.

'We should do lunch,' I said as she brandished her ticket at the barriers.

'You've got my number,' she said, with another Scarlett smile, and disappeared into the crowds. I watched her go. As did plenty of other men. I felt a burst of pride and swagger. She walked like a model. Her long dark ponytail swung slightly behind her, in time with her slim hips.

I ran an involved post-mortem as I walked home. I'd overspent, drunk too much on a stomach containing nothing but four crisps and a blini, burned my bridges with Amelie, wasted half a bottle of expensive champagne when there was perfectly good free beer down the road, and I'd told a dozen lies.

On the plus side, a model wanted me to call her to fix up a lunch date.

I was well ahead.

Work went on. Katerina was busy and so was I so we arranged our lunch date for a couple of weeks later. I didn't want to push too hard because she might think I was some desperate loser, near-virgin runner or something. Also, I didn't have any money.

I was awoken in my dingy little room one morning at 4.30 a.m. It was Roland at the studio.

'Morgan's not here,' he growled. 'She won't answer her phone.' This was a problem.

Edie Morgan had a BIG interview that day. The Chancellor's wife was coming in to talk about a revealing dress she'd worn to the party conference a week or so earlier. The dress had caused a minor storm, and better yet, it had been designed by Jane Macauley.

What the hell did he want me to do about it?

I asked, but using different words

'Get in a taxi and go to her house. Break in if necessary and get her here. Give her some coffee. Get her here by 6 a.m. Or you're both fired.'

I laughed.

'What's funny?'

'You're not serious . . . err . . . about firing us?'

'No.'

'Oh good.'

'Of course we wouldn't fire Morgan, just you.' Click.

Great. This had bad day written all over it in blue biro.

I made it to Edie Morgan's house in twenty-five minutes; I had to get money from the cashpoint for the cab. I'd claim it back from expenses later. I left the meter running and rushed up to the house. It was a huge, white town house in Holland Park, though the front garden was marred by a broken champagne bottle. Edie didn't answer the buzzer but I didn't need to break in as suggested as the front door swung open.

Calling out, I wandered in, nervously. Imagining the worst.

I found it in the sitting room. It was like a scene from some American college movie. Debauchery. Like the biggest student party you've ever been to but with organic carrots in the vomit.

There were half-empty bottles dripping wine on to the carpet, overflowing ashtrays and cigarette burns on the sofa. There were empty CD cases coating the floor and I really hate to see that. There were also a number of buff-looking young men sprawled about the place, all sacked out and some snoring.

I couldn't resist. I took out my camcorder and filmed the scene from the fourth circle of hell. Sweeping past a sofa, I caught sight of a pair of high heels still on a pair of feet. I went to check it out.

Target acquired. It was Edie.

I thought over the options. I could go and make some coffee and a bacon sarnie for her and maybe one for me too, and wake her gently with some fizzy water and a couple of pills.

Or I could go nuclear and drag her out to the cab as is. The second option would be quicker, but this was our big talent, this was Edie Morgan, I couldn't treat her like that. She'd have me fired for starters.

I sent the cab away and went into the kitchen.

'Where the FUCK have you been, you little turdburglar!' Roland screamed as the cab stopped and I hopped out. A make-up girl ran around to the other side to where Edie was in the back, moaning softly. She was still drunk, despite my coffee and sarnies, which she hadn't touched (I ate them). She'd seemed confused and kept calling me Rudolph. Eventually she lay her head in my lap and went to sleep.

I shrugged. 'She wasn't co-operating, and besides, she's not in a fit state to be interviewing anyone today, I didn't see the point in—' but he cut me off, turning furiously.

'It's not your job to see any fucking point,' he fired at me, showering me with spit. 'I told you to get her here as quickly as possible.' He turned back and inspected his talent through the back window. Another assistant paid the driver and we helped Edie out of the cab, when she cried out and held up her hand against the weak morning sun like a vampire.

'Did you give her anything?' Roland asked.

'Yes, some aspirin . . .'

'No, I mean any Charlie? Jazz? Coke?'

I looked back, open-mouthed.

'Oh don't look so shocked, you little twit.' As the cab pulled off, he pulled a little bottle out of his coat pocket and tapped out a bit of powder on to his fingernail. Edie hardly opened her eyes, but snorted the coke readily enough. We all stood and watched, waiting to see what Frankenstein's monster would do next.

Edie snapped open her eyes, looked around at us all, then marched off towards the building. I swear she winked at me as she went past.

'We've got a show to do,' she snapped, 'come on.'

Roland stopped me. 'Go back to Soho,' he said. 'I don't want to see you here again this week. Send Rashid, he's a fucking idiot, but at least he follows orders.' And with that, he marched off after his buzzing talent and the fussing assistants.

I trundled back to Soho, wondering if I was going to be fired. But nobody ever mentioned it again. That's the industry. Scream a bit then forget about it. moveon.org.

I'd been staring at the blue slip for seven or eight minutes now, and it still wasn't making sense. The sick feeling was still thrashing about in my stomach, like a seal pup trying to escape a club-wielding Norwegian.

The blue slip was my pay advice. The thing that I couldn't grasp was why I had nearly two hundred pounds less than I thought I was going to get. I was still not entirely without hope that the accountant, Adrian, might have made a mistake and I could sort it all out by popping into his terrifyingly neat office and having a quick word.

But in my experience, in my life, on my planet, these things didn't turn out to be mistakes. The teacher hadn't made a mistake, that really was supposed to be a D next to your name. It hadn't just lost itself somewhere in your bag, your wallet had indeed been stolen. The girl snogging your best mate at your party wasn't someone who looked a little like the girl you fancied, it *was* her and she was using her tongue.

I popped in anyway, and Adrian took the slip to have a look. Adrian looked a lot like Minty from EastEnders. Everyone called him Minty behind his back, but never to his face. Best not to wind up the guy who sits in on all the pay-review panels, Rashid had said.

'This is your net pay here,' Adrian was saying, pointing to a disappointingly low figure.

'But if I'm paid £10,500 a year, then the monthly wage should be £875, no?'

'Gross, yeah. But this is net.'

I hesitated. Embarrassed to admit I didn't know what gross and net meant. But accountants were like doctors and priests, yeah? They wouldn't discuss personal stuff like that.

'Eh?' I said.

Adrian stared at me, I think he was trying not to laugh. 'Gross means before tax, net means after the Chancellor's taken his bit.'

It still took a second. Then the sickness hit again.

'Tax!'

'Oh yeah, baby.' Adrian smiled sympathetically. 'You forgot about the tax and national insurance. Looks like you're going to have to do your budget again.' He handed me the slip back. I felt crushed, as well as embarrassed. What the hell was I going to do? I shuffled off.

'Thanks, Minty,' I said glumly.

Later, in the pub with James and Rashid, I tried to forget all about it. A few pints weren't going to make much of a difference. 'I'll get them in, lads,' I said, striding up to the bar. 'Three Stella?'

'Yeah, but make my pint gross, rather than net, please?' Rashid said, accompanied by giggles from his idiot sidekick. So much for confidentiality. Perhaps Adrian was annoyed I'd called him Minty.

'How do you guys manage on the pay?' I said after the laughter had slowed.

'Well for one thing, we live a long way out of town, lot cheaper in the sticks,' said James. Rashid nodded as he pulled from his pint, a difficult operation.

'But then you have to pay a lot for transport,' I argued, trying to defend the idea that Soho could be affordable.

'Take the bus,' Rashid said. 'I live in zone 5, walk into zone 4 and take the bus from there. Much cheaper than the tube.'

I frowned. They were right, I'd have to move out. Give up my little room. I didn't like the idea, but I had no choice. I decided to speak to Ronnie about it when he came around for the rent tomorrow.

'Let's talk about something else,' I said. Wanting to put it out of my mind.

'That Elena's off on another bender then?' Rashid said.

I raised an eyebrow. Elena had been off for the last couple of days, leaving mountains of photocopying for me. I hated the photocopier, and it hated me. 'What do you mean, insert paper into tray 3? I've just put paper in, look, there it is, you stupid piece of junk . . . etc.'

'She's an alky, mate,' James added helpfully.

'This is why she's always off sick?' They nodded.

'Every few weeks she falls off the wagon and she disappears for three days.'

'Why doesn't Waters fire her?' I asked. 'Not like him to show compassion.'

'They go way back,' Rashid said. 'Used to get hammered

together. He cleaned himself up but she's still in the gutter. Feels responsible for her I reckon.' He finished his pint and, noticing James and I still had half a pint each, headed to the bar. 'I'm getting in a wedge,' he said.

For the uninitiated, a wedge is an extra drink bought separate to, and 'wedged' between, rounds to accommodate a particularly speedy drinking rate from one of the party. As James had explained to me at the pub after my first day, there are two types, the 'Open' wedge, bought with the knowledge of the others, and the 'Secret' wedge, bought and consumed while you were up at the bar getting your own round in. The secret wedge was usually a short, and was particularly useful when you didn't want to cause offence or when you were an alcoholic.

As I watched, Rashid had obviously decided he needed both barrels and got himself what he thought was a secret short to drink straight away and an open pint to bring back to the table.

I glanced around at the pub's interior. Afternoon light squeezed through the frosted panels at the front, illuminating specks of dust meandering through the air. Apart from the fruit machine there was nothing to suggest this pub had moved along with the rest of the world into the twentieth – let alone the twenty-first – century. Wooden floors, hard chairs and real ales. Things were OK here, I thought. Notwithstanding the money. Better than OK.

'How's your model?' James asked, grinning slyly as if reading my mind.

'She's just a mate,' I said, trying not to smirk.

I wanted him to ask again, but then we saw Piers, one of the senior producers, come into the pub. We all liked Piers, he was public school educated and fantastically polite, even when he was shouting at you. He stood looking about in confusion and we invited him over.

'Supposed to be meeting someone,' he said. 'Film-maker chap.' He looked around. 'Doesn't seem to be here, bit unreliable.'

'Have a pint while you wait,' James said and nipped off to the bar.

'Thanks, yes,' Piers said and sat down.

We liked hurling ideas for TV shows at Piers; he'd always listen politely and appear to consider the concept seriously, however idiotic the suggestion.

'What about a reality TV show involving homeless people? They get voted off the streets and into a hostel.'

'How about a game show involving asylum seekers? They have to answer questions about Britain and the one who gets most right is allowed to stay.'

'I had this idea about a drama series involving a crime-solving duo who just happen to be conjoined twins joined at the head. You could call it "A Problem Shared". The catchphrase could be, "Let's put our heads together and figure this out." '

Rashid tried him out with a new one.

'Hey, Piers, what about a fly-on-the-wall documentary about tube drivers?'

Piers raised an eyebrow in interest.

'You could maybe get some footage of people committing suicide, great TV!' he said, enthusiastically.

Piers frowned. James came back and had a go.

'What about a reality show where people have to be politicians and run the country for a bit? Couldn't be worse than the current lot.'

Piers didn't look impressed. He looked at me; 'What about you, err Dan? Got any ideas?'

I didn't, as it happened, but I didn't want to be left out. I thought quickly.

'Um, well I did have this idea about a pub,' I began, looking about.

He nodded. 'Go on.' I saw a sign on the wall of the pub claiming it had been around since the year 1663.

'Well it could be an old pub, built in the seventeenth century. And each episode of the programme, it's a period drama you see, could be set in the same pub but at a different time.'

Piers watched me intently. I thought furiously.

'So in the first episode, everyone wears wigs and takes snuff and that and maybe they get caught up in the Great Fire and have to rebuild it. And then the next episode is in the 1700s and everyone has powdered faces. And so on through the centuries and the last episode is set today.'

'And would you use the same actors playing different characters?' Piers asked.

That was a good idea. 'Exactly,' I said quickly. 'You could even have regulars, played by the same people and exhibiting similar characteristics throughout history.'

There was a silence at the table.

'That's actually a good idea,' said James, sounding surprised.

I was surprised too.

'I like it,' said Piers. 'Let me think about it.'

Then his film-maker turned up and he scuttled off.

We were quiet for a bit, thinking about what had just happened. Then Rashid said, 'This show of yours?'

'Yes.'

'Can I be in it?'

'Yeah, and me,' said James.

'Sure,' I said. 'Why not.'

I phoned Katerina that night. She'd been doing a catalogue shoot in Croydon and was exhausted.

'Croydon?' I said. 'Sounds nice.'

'Shut up, a shoot's a shoot.'

'Money good?' I asked – maybe I could ask her for a loan.

'No, the agency takes most of the money. We no-names get a pittance, though we do get lunch.'

'Which you don't eat?'

She laughed. 'That's right.'

'So when shall we meet?' I asked.

'Once I've finished the shoot – we've got a few more days.'

'OK, give me a call.'

'Will do.'

'Seeya.'

'Yeah, you too.'

A couple of days later Karen, the PR manager, grabbed me as I passed her cubicle.

'Dan, I have a job here that is really tedious and not very important so I'm giving it to you.'

'OK, I know my place,' I said.

'Good. Now, this company was supposed to deliver a vanload of drinks and snacks to one of our launch parties last year. It didn't arrive.'

'OK.'

'It took us a while to notice, and no one wanted to deal with it, so it kind of got forgotten.'

'You want me to sort it out?'

'The company tells us the goods were definitely picked, packed and put on the haulier's van, but they never arrived. We called the haulier but they claim they don't know anything about it. That's as far as I got.'

She handed me a purchase order, an invoice from the supplier, and the haulier's phone number.

'OK,' I said, 'I'll get on it.'

'Great,' she said, turning away. I realised she'd already forgotten about it. It was my problem now. If anyone asked her she'd just refer them to me.

I returned to Elena's desk and puzzled over the documents for a bit.

Waters popped his head out the door to his office.

'You,' he said.

'Mr Waters?' I replied, swivelling on my chair and trying to look like Michael J Fox in *Spin City*.

'Send some flowers to Elena at home.'

'Err,' I said, not at all like Michael J Fox who would have done it by now.

He gritted his teeth and clenched a fist. 'Use the company florist account. Her address is in her rolodex.'

I sent her gardenias. I like gardenias. They cost a bomb.

Katerina phoned the next day, as I was getting a bollocking from Waters. The phone was just going off in my pocket, the theme tune from *Dr Zhivago*. He either didn't notice, or didn't care. But I couldn't concentrate on what he was yelling; I just wanted to make the phone shut up, or him, but the phone was in my power.

'Hold on a sec,' I said to him, raising a hand. He stared in amazement as I pulled out the phone and turned it off.

'Sorry,' I said, 'go on.'

To his credit, he picked up where he'd left off and went at it for another couple of minutes. When he finished, I nodded briskly and said, 'OK, point taken,' and scarpered. I popped out on to the fire escape and listened to the voicemail.

'Hi, it's me,' she said. Me, she said. Me. 'Just thought I'd call and talk about lunch . . . err, that's it, call me.'

I decided I was going to leave her waiting for an hour but only managed half of that. I was too bored with work and couldn't get my mind off her. The thing I kept remembering about her wasn't her face, or her figure, it was the slightly crooked angle she'd stood at that night in Baa, popping one hip out a little in front. And at the same time poking one foot out. I guess she'd learned it at model school or wherever, and maybe it was affected. But it worked. Or at least it worked on me.

Now let's just stop a bit and go over what I thought about Katerina. Obviously I fancied her. She was a little dull, and not super-bright. I knew that. I also knew that she wasn't a girl I'd want to settle down with. I wanted to *lie* down with her, I wanted to be allowed to say to people, 'This is my girlfriend,' when we met them. I wanted others to look at me with her and think, there's a guy who's got something, he must have money, or power.

And this is why I felt so confident with Katerina, it wasn't that I didn't care about her, that I had no *emotional investment* as my hippy English teacher used to phrase it. It was that I had some power in our relationship. It was power built on a lie, but it was no less real for that. The girls at school, or at college, were all two or three steps above me in terms of looks and confidence. They had the power and the freedom. I had Mum and a text message asking me to pick up some clingfilm on my way home.

Whilst Katerina was way out of my league looks-wise, for once I had something she needed. Contacts, position, insider knowledge. The ground had shifted and both of us knew where we stood.

'Are you around tonight?' she asked.

'Ahh, I have a thing, but it won't take long.'

'Wanna buy me dinner?'

No. I have no money. I want you to buy me dinner. Let's use your non-existent money.

'Sure. Let me choose where, though,' I said, gurning.

'You didn't like Baa?'

'It was OK, just a bit RAMMED,' I chortled.

'Yeah, maybe it was a little, shall I meet you at your place?' I'd made the mistake of telling her I lived in Soho.

'No, it's a mess, I'll meet you in the Ship at eight.'

'Cool, see you then.'

'See ya.'

I snapped the phone shut, grinning, and looked up to see Amelie sitting on the fire escape steps a few feet away, watching me. She hadn't been there before, surely? She pulled at a cigarette, watching me with interest.

'Your model?' she asked.

I nodded, feeling uncomfortable, but not knowing why.

'I'm not sure she's right for you, Dan,' she said, frowning.

'I'm sure she's not,' I agreed, looking her in the eye and challenging her to say something else.

'Come on.' She stood and flicked the butt over the side. 'You're coming to the studio with me.'

I raised an eyebrow.

'Waters wants me over there and told me to take a runner – you're it.'

She swished past and I followed, thinking about power.

* * *

I liked being at the studio. In Soho I felt just like an office boy, here I was part of the glamorous world of TV. Edie Morgan was on the couch interviewing a minor politician trying to rebuild his career after some sexual indiscretion, the details of which he was a little vague about in his heartfelt apology.

Amelie was there organising a group of models on behalf of Jane Macauley who intended to show up at the last minute. She was in the dressing rooms and kept popping out to ask me to find people and get things from them. She also made me get her coffee. But as the morning wore on she got bored with making her point and stopped demanding stuff. I settled on a spare chair in a dark corner and watched. I also surreptitiously filmed various people from time to time.

It seemed to me to be organised in concentric circles. At the very centre was the presenter and her guests, or 'talent', always said with a hint of irony. Around them were the producers, stage managers, floor managers and cameramen. Outside that circle were the lighting guys and the sound guys, and in the outer circle were the stagehands and the support people, like make-up, researchers and runners.

After filming, Amelie and I went for a walk by the canal. 'I know a good place for lunch,' she said, 'we can put it on expenses.'

'Great!' I said. 'Do you always get lunch on expenses?'

'No. Only on days when I have to go somewhere. The rules are a bit vague about whether the studio counts as away, but everyone bends the rules a bit and no one's ever said anything. Take what you can get away with, I say.'

'Smash and Grab,' I said quietly.

'Eh?'

'Nothing.'

We walked on, the chill breeze flicking the surface of the leaden canal, making it shiver.

'Do you just want Katerina because she's a model?' Amelie asked.

I paused to collect my thoughts, taken aback. 'No, I just want her because she's a girl. And she showed an interest in me. That's not usual for me.'

'There must have been girls back in Keenham?' she said, getting a little personal, I felt.

'I had a girlfriend, Kate,' I said. 'We went out together for a while . . .' I drifted off.

'It didn't work out?'

'No.'

'Why not?'

'I don't want to tell you.'

'OK, fair enough.'

In truth, Kate had dumped me very quickly, and the day after we had done it. Or nearly done it. But let's not go there.

'So tell me about Katerina then,' she said. We'd reached the pub now and she ordered us bottles of lager and a burger each. It was one of those places you suspect only has people in it at lunchtime and only then because there wasn't anywhere else.

I shrugged. 'What do you want to know?'

I actually *wanted* Amelie to ask about her. I wanted to show off a bit, to talk about how I was going out with a model. In the back of my head was another angle too. I wanted to make Amelie jealous. But I tried not to think about that.

'What do you see in her?'

I shrugged again, I'd have to stop that. Start thinking more.

'I haven't analysed it. We've only been out once, properly.'

'But you're seeing her again?'

'Yeah, why not. She's nice, she's pretty, and she seems to like me.'

'Are you sure she's not just using you?'

I stiffened. What did she know?

'How would she use me? What can I give her?'

Now it was Amelie's turn to shrug.

The conversation was interrupted briefly as the waitress arrived.

'Here's your meals for yourselves,' she said, perkily. 'And here's your cutlery . . . for yourselves. Anything else I can get for yourselves today?'

'Thanks, no,' Amelie said, shortly.

I was a bit offended by Amelie's comments. Was she suggesting that Katerina could only be interested in me if she was hoping I could help her out, career-wise? That might be true, but it wasn't very flattering. I decided not to pursue the question as I didn't really want to know the answer.

We talked about other things, work gossip mostly. Bryone was sleeping with Dougal from the gulag apparently. James had been arrested in Hackney last Friday after falling through a shop window when drunk. He hadn't told me this. By mutual, unspoken consent, we'd decided Katerina was a subject off the menu for now.

'Come on,' she said once we'd finished. 'We've got to get back to the office.'

Having being in London six weeks or so, I figured I'd better send Mum some confirmation that I still existed. She left the occasional message for me but I never quite seemed to get around to responding to them. So I made a video diary the next morning before work and sent that. Mostly a head shot on my balcony, I showed a few of the least dingy parts of my flat, and a few shots at work too.

Hi Mum,
Everything's going great here. Got myself a flat, with a fridge, let's have a look inside. Hmmm, some champagne, some beer, some wine. Some bread. Well what else does a growing boy need? Here are some shots at work. That's usually my desk, when Elena isn't there which is most of the time. That's where my evil boss Waters sits, he's the producer on GTV's morning show and the other fashion programmes.

This is my girlfriend, her name's Katerina. She's a model. She's really nice and very clever. Did I mention she's a model?

Anyway, things are going really well here. I'm assistant producer now. I've been pitching some show ideas to one of the senior producers. We'll see.

Well gotta go, got movies to make, love you!

And I kissed the lens and stopped the tape. In lo-res, it was small enough to email. I knew Mum would send it on around the world: 'Look at how well Bryan's done for himself!'

I just wanted them all to see Katerina, and how amazing she was. I wanted them to be impressed.

After sending the diary, I snuck out and headed down to the tube station. I intended to spend the day hanging about with a film crew in Ladbroke Grove. The show was a pilot for a new mystery series involving a time-travelling art historian. They weren't doing anything too exciting, just taking some establishing shots of outdoor locations in between hanging around waiting for the light to be right. Ninety-nine per cent of what happens in the TV industry is desperately dull, but I liked being on location. I spent most of the time getting coffee for people from the catering van, or popping off to the shops to buy tape, or pencils, or cigarettes.

My phone rang. It was Elena.

'Where are you?' she demanded.

'On location with the B unit.'

'What the hell are you doing there?' she spat.

What's it got to do with you, lady?

'Max told me they needed me.' This wasn't strictly true. I'd asked Max, the producer of this show, whether I could go; he'd shrugged and said 'sure' without even looking up from his computer.

'Get back here,' she croaked at me. 'Waters needs you.'

'Fine,' I sighed. I knew he wouldn't want me for anything important, or interesting. But that's the job. You do what people tell you.

I exited the tube at Tottenham Court Road, intending to walk down through Soho Square.

'Dan,' I heard. I spun.

'Hey, James, what's up?'

James was carrying a cardboard box; he showed me what was inside, eight or so bottles of wine.

'Having a party?' I asked, hoping I'd get an invite.

'Better than that,' he said. 'Come with me.'

We walked up the escalators, James barging past people in the way. He came up behind a barely-moving lady on the left-hand side.

'Can't you read?' he shouted in her ear; she jumped. He pointed to one of the ubiquitous signs saying 'stand on the right'.

'I'm walking!' she protested.

'That's not walking,' James said, shortly. 'That's . . . occasional stepping.'

She huffed and tutted but got out the way.

'Bloody pommies,' James muttered.

Outside we walked down into Greek Street and James

took us down a little alley to the back door of a restaurant. He kicked at the door.

A man dressed in chef's whites popped out.

'James, my man.' Then looking at me: 'Who's this?' He had a French accent.

'He's all right, this is Dan, he works with me.' The man nodded.

'This is Mick,' James said.

'Michel,' said Mick.

'Yeah,' said James absently.

'What have you got?' asked Mick/Michel.

James showed him. Mick shrugged.

'Table wine,' he said.

James sputtered. 'This is NOT table wine.'

Mick shrugged again, looking supremely uninterested. 'I give you tenner for the lot.'

James snorted. 'You and I both know you'll sell these to the punters for fifteen pounds a pop. This is good stuff.'

'How much you want, then?' Mick asked.

The alley smelled of urine and rotten food. It could have been New York. This is cool, I thought.

'Give us thirty,' James said.

Mick laughed. 'I give you fifteen.'

James picked up the box and walked off. I followed, uncertainly.

'Twenty,' Mick called. He wanted the wine.

'Twenty-five,' James called back, stopping, but not turning.

'OK.'

Later, as James stuffed the money in his back pocket, whistling cheerfully, I asked him where he'd got the wine.

'Leftovers from the party the other night. It pays to hang around till the end. You can pretend to be helping tidy and stick all the unopened ones into your bag.'

'I'll have to remember that,' I said, smiling. He looked at me and winked.

'Do you know what mag-op tape is?' Greg asked later that day, leaning over my (well, Elena's) desk. She'd gone home with a migraine, which was presumably the real reason she wanted me to come back. She wanted to go home and watch *Countdown* with a bottle of vodka. Greg was one of the sweaty technical geeks who worked in the back room. I had no real idea of what he did. He was just a fat geek to us.

'Yes,' I replied. 'They're not used any more though, we use . . .'

'DVDs, yes, I know that,' Greg said through gritted teeth. 'I work here too, you know.'

'Sorry,' I mumbled.

'One of our clients in Eastern Europe wants some film supplied on mag-op tape.'

'Why?' I asked, because I'm dumb like that sometimes.

He stared at me for a bit.

'I don't give a flying fuck why,' he said slowly. 'I just do what I'm told, then pick up my pay at the end of the month.

Why not do things the same way as me? It's preferable to being murdered with this,' he said, showing me an electrical cord he was carrying.

'OK, fine, whatever,' I said. 'You want me to find somewhere that sells mag-op tapes?'

'Now don't do that,' he said.

'What?' I asked. I could feel the smirks of the people within earshot, which was half the office because it had suddenly got very quiet. Rashid was openly laughing.

'Don't start using your initiative. Just do what I ask you, think you can handle that?'

'Sure,' I said, my face burning. 'What should I do?'

'Go to Mackenzie's on Lexington Street and buy thirty-six mag-op tapes, Rexell brand if they've got them. OK?' He was still staring at me. I squirmed under his sweaty, piggy gaze.

'Yeah, except I haven't got any money,' I said.

'Get some from petty cash!' he sputtered, astonished at my idiocy.

'No, I mean there isn't any in petty cash,' I said, 'Waters took it all for lunch.' Elena being away again meant I was in charge of the petty cash tin.

He leaned closer and looked like he was going to kill me. I shuffled back nervously on my chair. He smelled a bit of unwashed sheets.

'Wait here,' he said and disappeared. The room took a collective sigh of relief but sucked it all back in again a few minutes later when he reappeared with Adrian who handed me a credit card.

'Keep this. Lose it and we lose you, understand?'

'Yes,' I said, not sure I wanted it.

'The pin is written on this piece of paper, look at it.'

I did so.

'Remember it,' he said, and scrunched up the paper. 'Get receipts for everything and remember which client it's for, yes?'

'Yes.'

'If you have a receipt, you're fine. If you don't, you pay the money back, OK?'

'OK.'

And Adrian disappeared.

'I need them now,' the Fat Geek said, following him back to the Dungeons and Dragons Zone.

'Hi, Ronnie,' I said. 'Here's the cash.'

'Cheers, Maestro,' he said, taking what was left of my first month's pay. I'd bought a few cans of soup to get me by and was hoping for some free grub as the early-season parties started up. I intended to fill my pockets. I was already nipping into work early and drinking most of the milk some trusting soul left on the doorstep every day. I gave some to the homeless guy across the alley too. His name was Steve he told me one day, and Dave another. It may have been two different guys, but I don't think so.

He turned. 'Ronnie,' I said.

'Yup.'

‘I think I might need to move out, mate. Can’t really afford it.’

He shrugged and frowned sympathetically. ‘You signed a lease.’

‘Yeah, but . . . you won’t have any trouble finding someone else for this place.’

‘Sure, I don’t really care, but you won’t get your deposit back,’

‘That’s a bit rough, mate,’ I said, pleading, and realising I sounded like a whiny teenager.

‘Not up to me,’ he shrugged. ‘I just collect the rent.’ And he was gone, down to do battle with the drunks on the first floor.

Without that money, I couldn’t afford a deposit anywhere else. I was stuck here for six months. I sank down on the bed, my mind a blank. Looking for a plan. C’mon, Scheme-Boy, Captain Cunning. What’s next?

I checked my watch. Have to think about it later. Nearly eight. Time to go. Date with the Girl. The Model. Katerina. Oh yes.

I had a plan about tonight at least. I’d kept back a tenner, enough for a round at the Ship, then we’d go to Pollo, a cheap cafe with enough Soho atmosphere to make it seem as though it wasn’t the cheap option. I had a small overdraft facility on my current account; I’d whack the meal and a bottle of wine on the plastic. Then I’d make a move. If she rejected me, then I could call a blessed halt to the whole situation, walk her back to her train and say goodbye for ever.

If she didn't reject me, well, then I was quids in and I shouldn't need to spend any more. I couldn't bring her back here of course, but we could maybe go to her place, and if not, I'd play the slow-and-steady card and leave her wanting more.

It was a perfect plan that wouldn't bankrupt me and might just lead to me having sex.

4

Int. low light. Strobing reds, thumping drum and bass soundtrack. Close, claustrophobic atmos. Crowds of dancing extras. Camera sweeps and raises on gantry then swoops to close-up of boy and girl embracing in the centre of the dance floor, untouched by extras.

I thought back, trying to remember the details of the plan, six hours later as Katerina and I kissed on the dance floor of Klubb, the most fashionable nightclub in Europe at that moment (though it's now called Gold and plays cheesy eighties tunes to crusties in their thirties.)

She'd got her name on the guest list somehow and after toying with her salad and ignoring the wine I poured for her at Pollo, she'd taken me straight there and breezed past the shuffling lines of clubbers. The bouncers checked a list and we were in.

My. God. The drinks were expensive. I had to wait so long at the bar I thought maybe inflation had kicked in. I'd nearly forgotten what I came for by the time I was served. Oh yeah, CHAMPAGNE! Cos that's what she'd asked for. Why on earth had I bought a bottle before? I should have told her I didn't drink. When I got back to her she wasn't there. I wandered around for a bit, feeling like an idiot with a bottle and two glasses.

I eventually found her ensconced on a comfy settee with a bunch of people she obviously knew.

'Dan! These are some friends, this is Blah blah, and that's Thingy, and this is Whatsit . . . etc.' Those weren't their real names of course. I don't remember what their real names were. And I don't care. They were all attractive. Or if they weren't they wore bizarre paisley clothes and ludicrous haircuts that distracted you from how unattractive they were. Their bearing was sourly confrontational and their very presence warned you off commenting on the curry-house pattern of their shirt fabric.

I was left to perch on the end of a couch arm, next to Whatsit, a huge blond bloke with the tightest shirt I've ever seen on anyone. He had muscles like pigs in a bladder. He ignored me, perhaps somehow sensing we'd have no conversation. I poured Katerina a glass and passed it over. Her chums were uber-hip. Talking in mumbles I couldn't hear over the thumping crap coming from the speakers.

All I could think of was how I was going to get out of this. I couldn't afford this. I was in over my head.

I looked at the bottle in one hand and the glass in the other. Well, that was one way to escape. I finished the glass and poured another, ignoring the raised eyebrow I got from Whatsername on the opposite sofa.

Beautiful people floated by, looking glamorous and

unapproachable. I didn't belong here. I wasn't beautiful. I didn't float. I was too approachable. Though no one approached.

Eventually Whatsit got up and went to the loo. I grabbed his seat, determined to defend it against all comers. If Whatsit tried to take it back I decided there'd be a vulgar scene. Katerina smiled at me and I poured her more champagne.

'Have you heard anything more about Paris?' she asked.

'Like what?' I replied, guardedly. I didn't like this subject, it worried me.

'Like whether you're going, and whether you might be able to get me into any good shows?'

'Well . . .' I said, uncertainly.

She fixed me with an impenetrable gaze. 'You do have the seniority to get me an invite to the show?' Was it a question? Or an affirmation?

So she'd decided on the open assault. I obviously wasn't taking the hint. I thought it over. If I said no, that was it. The night would be over, we would be over. I'd never have sex with her, or probably with anyone ever again. The advantage of that would be that I'd save loads of money on champagne.

If I said yes, I'd probably end up in debtor's prison, assuming they still had those, and my conscience wouldn't get any clearer, that was for sure. But if I said yes, she might sleep with me. She looked up at me and blinked slowly. And girls, here's a tip: If you want to look sweet and innocent and sexy and vulnerable at the same time, look up at a guy and blink slowly. Really, I mean that.

'Yes,' I said. A no-brainer. 'Sure I have the seniority, I can take you as my guest. I'm just not sure if I have the time to go myself.'

Genius. I'm a genius. I'm the Kaiser Soze of the Guild of Runners.

Then she smiled and said, 'Can I stay at yours tonight?'

And all was right with the world. Who needed money, or dignity, or self-respect, when Katerina asks a question like that?

But I couldn't take her to mine. I knew that. The gig would be up. She'd never sleep with me if she saw where I lived. Nonetheless, a man can't say no to a question like that. We're just genetically incapable of it. It would be like not banging your head when you get to the guitar riff in 'Bohemian Rhapsody'. Impossible.

'Sure,' I said, wondering how I could get out of it gracefully.

She asked me to dance and took me on to the floor and we kissed. Which was wonderful. Her lips were moist and her hips were surprisingly curvy for a size four. I could feel she was no choirboy. I haven't kissed many girls, and I don't really know if I'm doing it right, though what other way could there be? You just stick your lips against the girl's and mash them about.

I could feel her friends' eyes burning into my back and the world was as it should be; for one passing moment, all the planets were in alignment. I had what I wanted.

We stayed till the early hours then ditched her loser friends and went to an all-night café. I bought two overpriced Full English on my battered plastic and watched in agonies as she toyed with hers.

'Do you think I'm too fat?' she asked.

Danger. Danger!

'Are you asking me as a producer on a fashion show? Or as . . . something else?'

She smiled and didn't reply.

'It must be hard knowing what people are going to want – one day they want heroin chic, the next they moan how everyone's too thin,' I said, trying to weasel out of it.

'Where do you stand on thin models?' she asked.

'I try not to stand on them at all,' I replied. 'They snap easily.'

She laughed, she was beautiful. Then I thought of how I was going to get out of the taking her home thing. I jerked and reached into my pocket.

'Excuse me,' I said and pretended to read a text.

'I'm sorry, I have to go,' I said looking at her in dismay, which I didn't really have to put on. I was, how shall I put this, frustrated, but it wasn't all that bad. Now that I knew she wanted to sleep with me, that it was just a matter of time, I felt OK about the delay. I could arrange things properly, get a place sorted out, someone's flat, a B&B in the country. Maybe I could go down to hers on the weekend. Something would come up. As it were.

A tactical withdrawal was necessary now; the enemy was defenceless and could be picked off at the time of my choosing.

'Who's texting you at three in the morning?' she asked, reasonably.

'My boss,' I said. 'He's entertaining some clients and they've got themselves into a bit of a pickle. I need to go and help sort them out.'

She looked at me oddly.

'It's part of my job,' I shrugged. 'I need to keep the clients happy, and I always have to be on call, that's why I got the apartment in Soho.'

She didn't look as disappointed as I hoped she would. But it was late, she must be tired.

'I'll walk you to the train station,' I said.

'The last train's gone,' she replied evenly.

'Bollocks,' I said.

'It's OK, I can take a cab.'

I should have just kept my mouth shut, but it would have been a low act; I knew she didn't have much money, though more than me. And considering it was I who was welshing on the deal we'd struck back in the club, it would have to be me.

'Sure,' I said, 'I'll pay.'

'You don't have to do that,' she said, though her heart wasn't in it. We both knew I did.

'I'm really sorry about this,' I said.

She smiled. 'It's OK, maybe next time.'

'Definitely next time,' I replied, and my spirits took a spin, danced a jig and drank a Bacardi breezer.

I stopped at the cash point on Greek Street.

'Thirty pounds enough?' I asked, desperately hoping it would be.

'Sure,' she said.

But the machine wasn't having any of it. Cash machines, like flies, can spot bullshitters miles away. This one sneered at me.

INSUFFICIENT FUNDS

it blinked at me. I moved my body in front of the screen so she wouldn't see. What the hell was I going to do? There was nothing for it. I pulled out the GTV credit card. Adrian had given me the PIN.

Handing her the money I said, 'Can you get a receipt from the cabbie? I'll claim it back from the company.'

'OK,' she shrugged.

Some people have the ability to magic a cab out of nowhere. Tall, white, attractive girls, mostly. She was one of those people. And the cabbie was happy to go south of the river for her.

He was less happy about waiting for us to stop kissing though. We broke off and smiled shyly at each other.

'Bye, you,' she said.

'Seeya,' I said, feeling cheesy and just wanting her to go so I wouldn't say something gauche thereby reminding her I was still a child, really. A child who's slept with two women and one of those wasn't proper sex really. And neither was the other one if I'm being completely honest. But we don't say the V word around here. If you add up all the nearly-sex I've had, then I reckon I've done it around two and a half times. Though I don't think I was very good at it.

But while these idiotic thoughts were flapping through my head like insane bats wearing Halloween witches' costumes, she slipped gracefully into the black cab and was gone.

I dawdled back to the room, trying to think about kissing models, rather than INSUFFICENT FUNDS and receipts.

She called me the next day. *She* called *me*.

I took the call whilst wielding a cardboard tube. Most of the important people were out of the office and we were playing cricket in the gulag. The South Africans had discovered a sense of fun from somewhere and we were playing Colonials v Imperialists. The ball was made of an old computer mouse wrapped in parcel tape.

'Hello?' I said, swiping one-handed at a full-length delivery from Rashid, who fancied himself as a bit of a demon. The fielders were standing well back, some of them cowering behind desks.

'Hi there,' she said. 'Whatcha doing?'

'What am I doing? Waiting for your call,' I replied, cheesily. James, my batting partner, made sick-making noises.

Rashid bowled a beamer at my head and I cracked it stylishly into Adrian's office as Peter van Dyck launched himself over his own desk in an unsuccessful attempt to catch it.

'Doing anything tonight?' she asked.

'Yes I am.'

'Oh, what's that?'

'I'm meeting a beautiful girl and taking her to a launch party.'

Greg retrieved the ball and hurled it at me. I ducked gracefully and it hit James at the non-striker's end next to the fax machine.

'I see, do I know this girl?' she was saying.

Rashid bowled. Whack. The ball went sailing back over his head. I was on fire. I could knock 'em to the boundary and chat up models simultaneously and all one-handed. Call me Freddie.

'You've seen her around.'

'What's that noise?'

It had in fact been Dennis the IT manager/wicket-keeper farting loudly behind me. I decided it was time to wrap it up.

'Oh, we're shooting a new documentary series about violent storms. I'm working through some synthesised thunder claps.'

The boys fell about laughing, she must have heard.

'Oh?'

'Yeah, anyway, I need to get on. I'll meet you after work, yeah?'

'Look forward to it.'

'I'm looking forward to seeing you too.'

I hung up. Just in time.

'Look forward to this, you plank,' Rashid said and grunted as he unleashed a full toss at horrendous speed. I used both hands and hit it to his right and uppishly. Just at that moment, Elena appeared from the front office, chuntering to herself. The ball hit her full in the face and knocked her glasses off. I hid under a desk.

'What the hell was that?' I heard her screech.

'Cover drive,' James said.

'So how does it work? The modelling business?' I asked. Katerina and I were meandering through Camden Markets later on. She was looking for something to wear to the album launch party in Berwick Street I'd got us invites to. I was trying to find something I'd consider buying if I had any money.

'Well, young, unknown models like me have to find an agency. They parcel out catalogue work, or maybe ads, or stuff like wedding fairs or car shows. They put us up in accommodation but they keep a record of how much that costs, which we have to pay back when we're earning enough.'

'So until you make it big . . .'

'There's no money in it, no. The work I do doesn't quite pay off what I owe them at the moment, not when you consider rent, tube fares and food.'

‘So they pay for all that too?’

‘Yes, you can draw on expenses, but it all goes against your tab.’

‘Is catwalk modelling better paid?’

‘Only once you’re established. The big names earn thousands per day. A hundred thousand maybe, depends on the label. But they can get more than that for photo-shoots and campaigns, and astronomical figures for endorsements.’

‘So struggling models get how much for Paris fashion week?’

‘There’s a scale. My first show would probably only be a hundred pounds or so. But the one after that they have to pay more.’

‘And that’s the same whoever the label is?’

‘Yeah, but it’s better to be on the big name catwalks because if you model Gucci or Galliano or something, then everyone wants you and you can do more shows.’

‘I suppose you’re more likely to get your picture in the mags with the big guys, too?’

‘Exactly,’ she said, turning to face me. ‘I’d love to get into Macauley’s show, for example. That might get me noticed enough to get on a better show.’ She stared at me intently. Did she think I could get her on to Macauley’s catwalk? How the hell would I do that? I smiled.

‘I’m sure something will come up,’ I said, as blandly as I could. She grinned and kissed me, then skipped off to look at an accessories stall. Had I just made a promise?

* * *

The party was pretty good actually. It was made memorable by Edie Morgan's presence. As she usually had to get up at 4 a.m. to get from her Holland Park home to the East End by 5 a.m., she rarely ventured out at night. But the singer on the album was one of her mates, so she'd graced us with her presence. It soon became apparent that she'd taken something to help her stay awake, and by 10.30 she was steaming. She behaved appallingly. First she grabbed Piers' bum. Then, she clasped Rashid in a bear hug that unbalanced him and sent them both crashing to the floor. She made mooing noises all the way through the record producer's speech. Katerina and I loved it. I got some great footage, too.

'Wow,' Katerina said. 'She really knows how to party. This isn't the impression she gives out on morning TV.'

'She certainly does.' I looked around, we were alone. 'Check this out,' I said. I pulled out the camcorder and played Katerina the footage I'd taken at Edie's house the morning she didn't turn up at the studio.

'My God,' she said, giggling. 'How come you weren't hung over?'

I paused for a second. Katerina assumed I'd been at the party as a guest rather than as a runner just sent to pick up the talent. I didn't want to lie, but I could hardly explain why I had been there.

'I didn't drink too much that night,' I said. Well it wasn't a lie, I had only had a couple of pints at the pub with James and Rashid. I left it there.

I had to put the camera away then anyway as Piers came over to chat.

'That idea of yours, about the East End pub drama. Do you mind if I pitch that at the next editorial meeting?'

I was stunned.

'No, of course not,' I said.

'Great,' he said. 'Let's chat about it more tomorrow.' He left. Katerina was watching me. I tried to stay cool.

'What's this about?' she asked.

I shrugged as though it were nothing. 'Oh just a programme idea I've been working on. It's silly really.'

She made me tell her about it, as I'd hoped she would. I silently toasted Piers. His timing couldn't have been better.

Later on as we stood outside, saying goodbye to Rashid and James, I was trying to work out a way of inviting myself back to see Katerina's flat. In the name of research, you understand. Unfortunately my plans were stymied by Roland, who saw me and stomped over.

'Get Morgan in a cab and get her home and into bed,' he snarled, as though I was responsible for the state she was in, presumably by holding her down and pouring champagne and coke into her mouth all evening.

'Shouldn't Amelie do that?' I said, seeing her wobbling out of the bar and thinking it might be better if a girl looked after Morgan, particularly after the last fiasco. Roland had apparently forgotten it was I who had screwed up last time Morgan got wasted.

'She's drunk as well.'

He was right, I realised as Amelie walked into a pot plant and staggered backwards.

'You do it,' Adrian insisted. He looked at Katerina. 'Does she work for us?'

'Yes,' I said.

'No,' Katerina said. Roland looked at me angrily.

'No, she doesn't,' I agreed. I'd been hoping that Roland might insist I took Katerina with me if he thought she worked there. As it was I had to say goodnight to her. The record company was paying for taxis for everyone so I didn't need to worry about that this time. Roland appeared from inside lurching along with a rolling Edie Morgan, who was singing a filthy, and probably libellous, song about a well-known TV personality.

'Call me,' Katerina whispered as she kissed me goodnight. I went a bit silly and couldn't think of what to say, then I turned and stumbled over to where Roland was trying to get the giggling Morgan into a minicab. I wasn't exactly sober myself.

'Is she gonna be all right?' the cabbie yelled, turning around. 'Blimey, is that Edie Morgan?'

'Yeah,' I shouted, climbing in the back. 'She'll be fine, just drive. Thirty-three Endsleigh Avenue, Holland Park.' I knew it well.

The cabbie grunted and took off.

Edie wasn't fine, not really. I had to give the cabbie my phone number and my contact details at work so he could send us the cleaning bill. My own clothes would have to make do with a premature launderette trip. Edie made me go through her bag to find her keys on her doorstep and while I did so she wandered off into the garden. I thought it was kind of funny and I couldn't resist taking out my camcorder and filming her in the orange streetlight staggering about the small patch of lawn before her two million pound West London home. It was hard to see her clearly through the viewfinder and it wasn't until a car drove past and illuminated her clearly for a second or two that I realised what she was up to. She was squatting on the grass having a pee. I snapped off the camera, giggling to myself.

I got her into the house and up into her room. All the time she was saying, 'You're a lovely boy, I do think you're lovely' and so on. She asked me to take her clothes off but I stopped after her shoes.

'Stay and have a drink,' she slurred.

'Err, well, maybe it would be best if you were to have a little snooze now,' I said. 'You have to be up early in the morning.'

'Oh fuck that,' she said, sitting up, suddenly sharp as a tack. 'I'm not going to work tomorrow. They can all go to hell.' Then she flopped back on the bed and spoke no more.

I suddenly realised I was starving. I'd eaten nothing but the odd canapé since breakfast, which had been someone else's cereal I found in a cupboard in the kitchen at work.

I went downstairs and stood in the kitchen looking at the enormous fridge. Edie had offered me a drink, after all. I was sure she wouldn't mind if I had a little bite to eat too, for my trouble.

I opened the fridge and gasped. She had everything. Meat, beer, vegetables, VEGETABLES. I'd forgotten what they looked like. Sod it, I thought, Smash and Grab.

I grilled myself an enormous steak, cooked some oven chips and opened an enormous packet of prepared salad. I found a nice-looking bottle of red in the wine rack and settled down to stuff myself. But first, I filmed it.

I also took my vomit-ey, fag-stinking clothes off and chucked them in Edie's washing machine. I put on a pink dressing gown I found in the upstairs bathroom and ate my steak, deliriously happy and bursting into giggles from time to time.

By the time I'd finished the bottle and done the washing up, I was very drunk and it was too late to get the tube home. Also, I was pretty sure there'd be difficulty getting Edie up at 4 a.m., just over three hours away, I decided to crash out on the sofa. I set the alarm on my phone before I sacked out. Tomorrow was going to be a long, difficult day.

I'd never been happier.

'He was in my house!' Edie screamed at Roland as the make-up girl wrung her hands over what to do with the disaster area that was the celebrity's face.

'He was trying to make sure you got home OK, and in to work OK this morning,' Roland said reasonably, trying to calm her down.

To be fair, I must have given her a shock when I went into her room that morning.

'Did you need to give her such a fright?' Roland asked, turning to me.

'She kept turning her alarm off,' I protested. 'I had to do something.'

'You leaped into the room squealing like a banshee,' Edie said. She hadn't called me lovely this morning. I'd been pretty harsh with her.

'That's an exaggeration,' I said.

Edie continued protesting but the make-up girl forced her into silence by plastering pancake batter around her withered jaw.

Roland took me away. I braced myself for the screaming fit.

He fixed me with the intense glare that was his trademark. 'Well done,' he said gruffly.

'Eh? I thought you were going to yell at me.'

'Why? You did exactly what you were supposed to, and you put yourself in an uncomfortable position for the good of the show. Keep it up.'

I smiled, deciding not to tell him about the 'comfortable' steak I'd eaten, or the luxurious bottle of expensive-looking wine. 'Thanks,' I said.

'Now get back to Soho. If you stay out of Edie's way for a few days she'll forget all about it.'

'OK, Roland, cheers,' I said and left.

My iPod played 'Crush the Losers' by Regurgitator on

the tube back into the West End.

I was back on top.

'I need you guys tomorrow night,' Amelie said, popping her head around the door to the fire escape. Rashid, James and I were in our 'office'.

'All three of us? Together?' James asked, smirking.

She sighed. 'From what I've heard, even all three of you together won't have enough to satisfy.'

'Well, even a 747 looks pretty small in the Grand Canyon,' Rashid said.

I didn't really feel comfortable being part of this and I couldn't think of anything clever to say.

'Free booze and food,' she said.

'We're in,' I snapped back. I was HUNGRY.

'We're looking after some clients,'

'Oh God,' said James.

'Not the Germans?' said Rashid.

Amelie grinned.

'Why can't we look after the Spanish? Those girls are gorgeous.'

'Do you think you'd be given the job if it was the Spanish?' Amelie asked. 'Waters would do it himself.'

'What's wrong with the Germans?' I asked, innocently.

'They drink too much, then they always insist we go and find some girls,' Rashid answered.

I shrugged. 'Sounds like your thing, especially if it's on the company.'

'Yeah, but they always make us go and chat up the girls, then they paw them and get us into a fight with the bouncers, or the girls' boyfriends, or both.'

'How often does this happen?' I asked.

James dragged on his butt and flung it over the side. 'Two or three times a year. They love us, apparently.'

'One of 'em loves me, I know that,' Rashid said miserably.

'Lobby bar of the Carlton, 8 p.m. tomorrow night, all three of you,' she said finally and was gone.

'Yeah, hi. I'm trying to track a delivery that's gone missing. Order number Q23657.'

'OK, hang on.'

Clicking of keys.

'Yeah, that was collected by Dangerfield Vans on September 13th at 10.32, signed for by Rob.'

'Thanks.'

Click. Dial.

'Dange-field?'

'Can I speak to Rob please?'

'Hold on.' Beep beep.

'Hello?'

'Rob, this is Dan Lewis from GTV, you collected some goods for us on the 13th September and were supposed to deliver to the Goolie bar on Greek Street in Soho, but the drinks never arrived, I'm just trying to track them down.'

'Oh yeah, I remember that. Hold on.' Clickety-click.

See, that's how easy it is to sort things like this out. What the hell was Karen doing all that time? A couple of phone calls and bang, sorted. I popped my feet up on Elena's desk and picked my teeth with her letter-opener.

'Yeah,' Rob said. 'The address was wrong, there was no bar by that name on Greek Street. Brought them back to the warehouse.'

I looked at the address on the docket and googled Goolie's. The address was indeed wrong. The Goolie bar was on Greek Street, but way down the other end.

'Did you not have a phone number to call?'

'Yeah, a mobile. Contact name James. I phoned and left a message but no one ever got back to me.'

That figured. James was useless.

'Oh, so do you still have the goods?'

'They'll be in the undelivered stock room, it's a bit of a mess. I suppose I could have a look but there's a charge for storage and for any extra delivery.'

'Hmm, hold on.'

I covered the receiver while I thought it over. Waters would never agree to pay the extra charge. No one really cared about the stuff. If anyone asked, I could just pretend I hadn't got any further with it than Karen had. I looked around. No one was in earshot except Amelie, who was slumped on her keyboard having had an awful morning trying to organise the Paris trip.

'Rob?'

'Yeah?' He sounded impatient. Wanting to get back to his sweet tea and the *Daily Mirror*.

'Do you know what was in the consignment?'

'Err, no I don't remember.' He sounded bored.

I picked up the purchase order and read it out.

'One case of scotch, six cases of champagne, four cases of red wine, four cases of white wine, six times twenty-four cartons of French lager, plus assorted crisps and nuts including four packets of Twiglets.'

'OK?' He still hadn't got it.

'If you find it, you can deliver half to me, and keep the rest for yourself.'

There was silence.

'Otherwise I get you to deliver it all to the office here, we pay the extra costs to your company and neither of us gets anything.'

'What's the address?' he asked. He'd got it now.

I gave him my address.

'I'll see what I can do,' he said. 'I'll only be able to look after hours, or else they'll ask me what I'm doing. Might have something next week?'

'Fine,' I said. I gave him my mobile number and hung up. Then I stood and jumped up and down a bit to celebrate my own cleverness.

Smash and Grab.

'Hello?'

'I'm in town tonight, meeting some mates. You around?'

'Whatsit and Thingummy?'

She laughed. 'No. Some real mates, from college.'

'What college did you go to?'

'Jane Grover's Modelling Academy.'

'All your friends are models?'

'Yeah.'

It was really hard to say no to this girl.

'I can't, I'm babysitting some Germans tonight,' I said, kicking the wall in annoyance.

'Oh,' she said. She sounded so disappointed.

'I'm sorry, I'm not blowing you off, it's really important this thing.'

'OK no problem, I was just hoping we could talk about Paris . . .' She tailed off. Where was she going with this Paris thing? Was she expecting me to get her on to the model list for the show? If so why didn't she just ask?

Then something occurred to me. 'Hold on,' I said and hit the hold button to give myself time to think.

A plan was forming in my mind, despite my efforts to stop it. It wasn't a particularly complicated plan. You can probably guess what it was.

I picked up again. 'Keep your phone on, I'll give you a call later tonight and arrange to meet up somewhere. These Germans I'm looking after might be worth you and your friends meeting.'

'Great!' she cried. 'Who are they?'

I had no idea. 'I'll fill you in later . . .' I said, '. . . matron.'

She giggled as I hung up.

I grinned. Feeling evil, and clever.

* * *

'Tea!' Max yelled at me as I walked back in from the fire escape.

'Yes please,' chorused half a dozen voices.

I didn't mind making the tea. At first I'd struggled to remember how everyone had it – what the hell happened to white with one? That was how everyone I knew back home liked it. These days it was all fruit teas, and herbal teas and black tea with lemon, and decaff this and half-caff that. Rashid had shown me an easy way to remember.

Melody Smellodie likes it fruity
Paul with red cheeks likes it weak
Michael White takes it black
Lovely Jeannie likes it creamy
The fat girl in the sales department takes it skinny
Stupid Max has big cup with cracks
Elena has it white with one sugar and a gob of spit.
I never forgot the last one.

The next evening. Rashid, James and I strode confidently into the lobby of the Carlton like a half-pack of Reservoir Dogs.

'OK, guys,' I'd explained as we walked up St Martin's Lane. 'Now when the girls arrive, remember we aren't runners, we're Associate Producers, the Rat Pack. Young Turks. We're going places.'

'Without running,' Rashid said.

'That's right. We're walking briskly and with purpose, not running. We have other people to do that for us.'

'Aaaagghh!!!' came a hoarse roar from the bar as we entered. A stereotype huge blond German came rushing towards us. James groaned as he was picked up and given a bone-crushing hug.

'Jaaaames!' he cried, then saw Rashid and gave him the same treatment. Then he spotted me.

'Who's this bastard?' he roared, delighted.

'Dan,' James said grumpily, adjusting his clothes.

'My name is Hans!' the Aryan said, grabbing my hand and crushing it without offering an explanation. My knees buckled a bit.

I stared at him suspiciously. 'Are lots of German really called Hans?' I asked. 'I always thought it was just one of those cultural myths, you know, like all Italians live with their mum, and all Russian are drunks.'

'But it is true,' he cried. 'All Russians drunk like bastards!'

Three other Germans arrived from their table. Less buff, but just as enthusiastic. I liked them.

'I'm Dieter,' one said.

'Helmut,' added the third.

'Colin,' the fourth said, puncturing the stereotype somewhat.

'Drinks!' cried Hans, clapping his hands together. I beamed and held up the credit card.

'We'll get these, fellas,' James said.

James and Rashid loosened up soon enough. The drinking potential of these guys was enormous, and we three runners struggled manfully to keep up. After a few pints, Hans insisted that we head off to a WONDERFUL restaurant he knew.

'We will pay, you got the drinks!'

We tottered along behind them out the door when I was accosted by the barman, who asked me to sign the bill.

As we walked down the street, Hans with his arm around Rashid, James and I whispered together.

'So these guys buy our programmes and then remake them in Germany?'

'Yeah, or else they just buy the film and dub it into German.'

'Do they buy any of our fashion programmes?'

'Err yeah, I think they take *How to Wear What You Really Shouldn't Be Wearing.*

'So why do they need to come here?'

'They don't, it's just an excuse to get away from the Frau for a bit and have a piss-up. Perks of the job, mate. The whole industry's this way. It's how things are done.'

'Suits me,' I replied.

'There's worse jobs,' he agreed.

Dieter sprang out at us from the wall he'd hidden behind. 'Hahhh!' he said in a pirate voice.

'Jesus Christ!' James said lurching back in shock, smoker's nerves shot to crap.

I fell about. Tonight was going to be fun.

Over dinner I quizzed Dieter on what exactly it was they did.

'We run some TV channels. We make programmes, or buy programmes,' he said vaguely.

'Programmes about fashion?' I asked.

'Yes. We have a channel devoted to fashion programming. We will be at Paris filming there, like you I think. Will we see you there?'

'Maybe,' I said. 'Do you go to all the parties?'

His eyes lit up. 'Sure we do. We get passes. Hans is well known and pulls favours so he gets us access-all-areas passes. Organiser's passes. You can go to all the shows, backstage and also the parties. So much fun, so many beautiful women.' He slapped my thigh as he said this.

I thought this over. A couple of those passes would be a nice gift to Katerina. It might get her off my back about taking her there. I wouldn't even have to go myself, though maybe it would be a good opportunity if I could find the money.

I called Katerina around 9.45 p.m. when we'd finished the last of the naan and the Germans were discussing whether to order another round of pints or to head on to a club.

'Where are you?'

'In Gold-digger.'

'Meet me at Klubb in half an hour. I have some very drunk Germans who may be able to open some doors for you.'

Doors to their hotel bedrooms, I thought. I felt a bit guilty about setting them up like this, but surely this was what it was all about? Networking, schmoozing. Making connections with people who may be able to help you, and partying a little at the same time. All at someone else's expense, of course. These girls weren't innocents and could look after themselves. I reminded myself to get the cab receipt from Katerina too, Adrian would want that, though to which client I was going to charge it, I had no idea.

The Germans were still arguing about what to do.

'Hans,' I said, leaning over conspiratorially. 'I have some girls waiting at a club near here. You may be interested to meet them.'

His eyes lit up.

'Cheque please!' he bellowed at the waiter who nodded dispassionately, showing nothing of the relief he must have felt to get rid of this Anglo-Saxon party of losers.

Katerina waved across the dark room. I led the stumbling men over. I had felt a fish out of water the other night, but next to these guys, I bet I looked good on the dance floor.

Katerina had spun her magic with the sofa acquisition thing again. This time I paid more attention as she introduced us to her friends. Siobhan, Grace and Jamelia. They sounded like made-up model names to me.

I left them to it and wound my way to the bar holding the credit card in front of me like a pensioner with a bus pass. The plastic was an amulet, a grail. Carried before an army, a guarantor of victory.

A space opened for me at the bar as I approached. The

barmaid smiled at me. She had great teeth and a cute little ponytail. This was like a Carling ad.

I handed her the card. 'We're sitting over there,' I said, pointing. 'Can I open an account?'

'Sure,' she said and checked a list. 'You're number one.'

'I certainly am,' I said, trying to control my smile.

'What can I get you?' she asked.

'Champagne, please. Three bottles and . . . eleven glasses.'

'I'll bring them over,' she said, flashing me those teeth again.

I returned, victorious, to find the party in full swing. The Germans were hilarious. Their chat-up technique consisted of extraordinary boasting.

'I was German champion bodybuilder in 1993,' Helmut told Grace, who giggled.

'I once was married to a famous German pop star, very beautiful, very rich,' Colin said to Jamelia. 'I left her.'

Hans was trying his luck with Katerina, I looked on, confident and superior.

'I run a TV station in Germany,' he said.

Katerina sparkled and poured him some champagne as he leaned back into the cushions, bloated and shiny with sweat.

'You are very beautiful, are you a model?'

'A TV presenter,' she said, touching his leg as she leaned over to put the bottle back on the table. He stared down her top as she did so and I could see she wasn't wearing a bra.

The Jealousy Gnome popped his head up and poked me with the Spear of Worry. She's such a liar, I thought. Some people.

He leaned close to her and I did the same, anxious to hear what he was promising her.

'Anytime you like, call me up, I put you into a programme on German TV. Very popular. Beautiful girls. Lots of money.' He handed her a card, which she took, to my annoyance.

'I am a writer,' Dieter told Siobhan. 'I write poetry.'

'Does that pay well?' she asked, absently.

'No, this job pays well, I am very wealthy, but the poetry I do because of love.'

Siobhan's nostrils flared. Though whether it was because of the money or the poetry I didn't know.

James and Rashid were chatting quietly. I shifted over to them. 'All right, lads?'

'Who are these girls?' they asked.

'Just some contacts,' I shrugged. 'Should make your job easy, yeah?'

James nodded, staring at Siobhan. 'Have you got any more?'

'Not tonight, but we'll see what we can do next time,' I said, big-heartedly.

Three hours later, the party had moved back to the hotel. The Germans had four interconnecting rooms and there was much running back and forth bouncing on beds.

On the way in I'd stopped at the desk and ordered six

bottles of champagne. Amelie had told me that we were supposed to be paying for the entertainment, though not the rooms. I gave the pretty receptionist the card and told her to hang on to it in case we wanted more drinks.

Up in the room, MTV blared from the telly and we'd all ordered from room service. Helmut had found himself a bottle of Scotch and had Grace sitting on his knee. He looked very pleased with himself. Colin was chasing a shrieking Jamelia throughout the suite. Dieter and Siobhan were pillow-fighting.

I pulled the camera out and filmed the chaos, delighted.

James and Rashid had accepted they weren't going to get any tonight and had decided to drink their way through till dawn. James lurched over to me. 'Where's your girlfriend?'

I looked about. Katerina had indeed disappeared. As had Hans. I wandered through into the next room; there was no sign of them. Then into the final room. Again, it was empty, and I turned to go, when I heard a giggle coming from the bathroom. I wandered over and stood outside. Listening.

More giggles. What the hell was this? My stomach lurched. Suddenly I wasn't having fun any more.

Then voices. My drink-pickled brain reeled slowly at what I heard.

'You want more?' Hans' voice, sounding strained.

'Yes,' Katerina replied.

Then a thud. A hand against the mirror? My weird imagination came up with an image of Kate Winslet in *Titanic*.

The Jealousy Gnome rummaged through my insides, looking for something. Then I shook my head. How was this happening? Was this happening? Katerina couldn't possibly bring herself to . . . not with Hans? But what else could be going on in there? A surge of anger took control of my hand and I grabbed the knob. The door was locked.

'Hold on!' Hans cried. 'I'm in here.'

I said nothing, but left the room, forcing myself to smile as I re-entered the party. James eyed me curiously. I grabbed a beer and sat in the corner, fighting the urge to just run, run out of there and keep on running, back home. I wasn't in love with Katerina, I knew that, but it still didn't feel good.

She came back into the room, scanning for me. Our eyes met and guilt was written over her face with marker pen. She came over, smiling, and sat on my lap. I didn't want to touch her, but didn't want a scene either.

'Sorry about that,' she whispered, 'just trying to get my foot in the door.'

'Is that what they call it these days?' I replied, icily. She stared at me, concerned.

I was about to say something else. Something truly nasty, something that would have ended it once and for all. Something that I can't bring myself to repeat now. But then I saw something.

A few flecks of white powder on her top lip.

It wasn't sex! It was drugs.

That was all right then.

A flood of relief washed the protesting gnome away in an instant. No matter that my girlfriend was a druggie. No matter that she was using him, and probably me, to get ahead. No matter that she was a liar. None of that was important.

She wasn't shagging the German.

I had another beer to calm my nerves. The party went on. I remembered my camera and got it all on film. Dieter and Siobhan canoodling, then disappearing into another room, holding hands. Colin slapping Jamelia on the arse. Helmut throwing peanuts into Grace's cleavage. Hans wrestling Rashid to the bed and grabbing his crotch before James pulled him away. He treated it all as a huge joke but I began to feel uncomfortable. The tape ran out and I went to my bag to change it for a fresh one.

Katerina came with me and put her arms around me as I stood. She'd hardly left my side since the incident in the bathroom; she was trembling a little as I held her.

'Do you want to go?' I asked.

She nodded. 'We've got to get the girls out, these men are starting to get frisky,' she said.

But then we were interrupted by a scream from next door. 'Shit,' I said softly. Suddenly this all felt wrong. And I was responsible for it. I was closest and rushed in.

Siobhan was standing by the bed, holding her torn dress against her chest. Dieter was laughing. 'You wanted it, you little bitch,' he said. Then something in German that made Helmut and Colin laugh. The three of them went through to the next room together.

'He tried to make me . . . make me . . .' But Siobhan didn't finish, couldn't bring herself to say what Dieter had tried to make her do. Jamelia and Grace led her to the bathroom. Katerina turned off the music and began collecting bags and coats. James and Rashid stood by looking useless.

Hans came up beside me. He noticed the camera in my hand. 'What is this? You are spying on us?' He spoke quietly so the others wouldn't hear.

'No,' I said shortly, feeling suddenly sober. 'I always carry my camera, I make films.'

'And what are you going to do with this film?'

I shrugged, disgusted that he was concerned about that rather than the behaviour of his colleague.

'Maybe you could give me the tape?'

I was happy to give him the tape. There wasn't anything on it after all. The good stuff was in my bag. But I didn't really feel co-operative. I didn't say anything, just fixed him with a judgemental look. He shifted uncomfortably, then thrust out his huge chest at me, fronting it out.

'Perhaps there is something I could give you in return?' he said, trying to smile warmly.

And almost without thinking, I said it.

'Can you get me two organiser's passes to the Paris fashion week?' I said, astonished at my own brazenness.

He thought for a bit, then smiled and shrugged. 'Of course, this is easy for me.'

'Great, send them to me at the office, and I'll send you the tape.'

I turned to go but was prevented by his claw-like grip on my arm. It hurt. I turned back, suddenly feeling less confident and wondering if I'd got in a little deep here.

I was dimly aware that the others had made their way through to the other room, leaving us alone.

'Give me the tape now, I will send you the tickets,' he said.

I stared at him. At that moment, all I wanted was to be out of the room. I didn't give a damn about the tickets.

'OK,' I said. I opened the camcorder and gave him the tape, hoping he wouldn't check it. He'd see immediately I hadn't used any of it yet. But his eyes remained fixed on mine. He snapped off the head guard and ripped out a stream of tape.

'*Danke*,' he said quietly.

'*Bitte*,' I forced out. Then his grip relaxed and I tried not to run out the door.

The others were waiting in the corridor and we got the hell out of there. In the lift on the way down, I said, 'Should we call the police?' They looked at me as if I were mad.

'Dan,' James said. 'We got out of it OK, let's just drop it and be more careful next time.'

I shrugged, feeling that we were doing the wrong thing, but not wanting to rock the boat considering I'd effectively just blackmailed a German film producer.

I put the girls into a taxi and asked Katerina to get a receipt. 'Sure, sure,' she said, absently.

‘You did get one the last time, yeah?’

‘Oops,’ she said, crinkling her chin prettily. I sighed inwardly – looks like I was paying for that one.

The car sped off and James, Rashid and I went to a twenty-four-hour pub to calm our rapid heartbeats with a pint and a whisky chaser.

Rashid paid for once.

5

Int. Day. Busy office scene. Extras walking rapidly across shot carrying papers etc. FX phones ringing, hum of conversation, clacking of keyboards. Cut to back office. Dan sits at a quiet desk picking up a phone.

I phoned Katerina from the back office the next day.

'Are you OK?' I asked.

'Sure,' she said. 'Why shouldn't I be?'

I paused, making sure I was remembering last night's events correctly.

'Well . . . last night was a bit. . . .'

'Oh that?' she laughed casually. 'That sort of thing happens to us all the time. That's the industry, Dan.'

People kept telling me the most appalling behaviour was part of the industry. Was I the only one with a conscience? Or was I just naive?

I snapped back into producer mode.

'Sure, I know, it's just that I feel responsible, I was worried about you.'

She was quiet for a few seconds, then: 'It was just a bit of charlie, Dan.'

‘Hey, I know, I know,’ I said. ‘I don’t have a problem with that.’

‘I don’t do it often, you know,’ she said. ‘He just asked me and I didn’t want to disappoint him, you know? I thought he could get me some party invites to Paris . . .’

‘I can get you those.’

She was silent.

‘I’ll get them for you. I said I would.’ Was this our first fight?

‘OK, Dan, I’m sure you will.’

‘Are you around tonight?’ I said. ‘Maybe we can meet near you, I’d like to see your flat.’

‘I’m off for a photo-shoot in Leeds today,’ she replied a little quickly. ‘Didn’t I tell you?’

‘No.’

‘I’m going with Siobhan, it’s underwear.’

‘Really?’ I said, sitting bolt upright. ‘What catalogue?’

She laughed. ‘I’m not telling you. Anyway, why do you want to see pictures when you can see the real thing?’

My jaw dropped. Across from me, Greg was watching my face with interest. I shut my mouth with difficulty.

‘When . . .?’ I said.

‘When can you see the real thing? How romantic,’ she said.

‘No, I mean when can I see you again?’

‘I’m back in London on Thursday, but I’ll be tired, maybe Friday?’

‘Great!’ I said enthusiastically.

'Maybe we could go to yours, my place is a bit of a dump,' she said.

I considered it for a second, but then rejected the idea. She'd back off if she saw it.

'Hm, mine is still a building site, I'll sort something.'

'Seeya then,' she said.

'Seeya,' I said and hung up. Greg eyeing me suspiciously.

I wandered into the editing suite, knowing if I went back out to the front office Waters would grab me and ask me to do something mindless. I wanted to do my own mindless things. David was the humourless IT guy who never ever left except to tinker with people's computers and be really abrupt with the owners. He was footling around with some gutted electronic device. In the corner of the room was a pile of middle-aged laptops, slightly foxed.

'David?' I asked.

'Yes?'

'What are those laptops doing there?'

'Nothing.'

'Can I borrow one, for home use?'

'To do work?'

'Err, yes.'

'What's your departmental code?'

'65.'

'OK,' he said, noting this down in his humourless, South African way.

Why are all IT guys South Africans? If I was South African, I wouldn't mess about with computers. I'd go to the beach. Maybe that was why all South African IT guys were losers. Maybe the cool South Africans were all at the beach. Only the geeks came over here and made piles of money. And then they probably went home intending to laugh at the cool beach guys. But the beach guys probably just said, 'Whatever.' Because it takes more than money to be cool.

That was easy, I thought, helping myself to an old powerbook. Old, but still considerably more powerful than anything I'd had before. Editing would be a dream with this thing.

As I was leaving, David spoke up. 'Lose it and it comes off your departmental budget. Waters OK with that?'

I thought for a bit. 'Sure,' I said. In for a penny and all that. And after all, Amelie had told me that everyone did this sort of thing.

I got back to my desk to find the phone ringing. It was the Carlton.

'Mr Lewis? We're still holding your company credit card here.'

'Oh hell, sorry, I completely forgot to grab it on my way out.' I'd had other things on my mind, of course.

'That's OK, sir, but there are some charges on the card and we need your signature.'

'Sure, sure, no problem,' I said vaguely. As it happened, I wasn't in any hurry to collect the card. If I didn't have it in my possession, I wouldn't be tempted to use it on things I shouldn't. I decided I'd leave it another night and collect it at lunchtime tomorrow.

* * *

When I got home that night, I spent the evening importing the video files I'd been taking since I arrived in London. There were hours of it. The laptop had a huge memory but even so I nearly filled it.

My phone rang once but I ignored it.

I started cutting crap, trying to reduce the size of the files and get rid of unnecessary footage. Establishing shots of Soho, the office, the flat. I kept the important, the best, shots and canned the rest, can't be sentimental. Those shots of Amelie I'd taken when she wasn't looking, she looked like she was working but as I panned around her you could see she was playing solitaire. I kept a bit of that for a laugh. I also kept the money shot in the toilets of the launch. And the Morgan footage of course.

Then I set about making a lo-res video small enough to send home and to Lucy. I hated writing letters, video was so much more immediate, and you could adapt it to say pretty much what you want anyway.

I plugged myself into the iPod. It kicked into Hole's 'Celebrity Skin' and I cranked up the volume to mask the moans of the drunks below and the hoarse calls of the street-trash outside. My immediate neighbours were quiet, mostly, but there was plenty of ambient sound nonetheless.

I checked the clock (which ticked perfectly, thanks for asking) when I'd done. 3 a.m. Nothing makes time fly like editing. I was exhausted, aching, and felt like I'd poured out all the stress, all the tension, all the worry that had been building up for weeks. The end result ran for a little over two minutes and had a grungy indie soundtrack I'd pulled from unsigned.com. It began with a blurred snap on the train, then me pulling a face at Aunt Mouldy's, then freeze-frame shots of me walking over Battersea Bridge. Then Amelie's legs in the reflection of the chrome door of the office. A shot of Waters stalking around the office. James and Rashid beered-up and lairy, my room, Wardour Street. Then Katerina. Timed perfectly, the music softened and slowed and I subtly slowed the playback speed as well, giving her a more languid air. The graininess of the stock couldn't disguise her beauty but I'd gone for a reportage style, muted colours reduced further to near-sepia by the powerful software on the laptop. She was smiling at me in the shot; it had been the day we'd walked down through Camden. Before the party we'd walked by the canal and had fish and chips on a permanently moored boat-restaurant. I'd used my card to pay and charged it to Jane Macauley.

The film ended with a shot of me on my terrace with the rooftops of Soho behind me. I grinned and gave a thumbs-up, then swigged from a champagne bottle I'd swiped from a party the night before. From the angle I'd used, it looked like I was on a proper roof terrace.

At first I thought I'd give a voice-over, but I figured the images would speak loud enough so I didn't bother. I didn't have broadband of course, so I nipped back to the office to send the file from there. Even lo-res it was pretty massive and would take a minute or so to upload to my web space. There was generally someone there at the office all hours, the security guard and the cleaners if no one else. I sometimes popped in for a cup of coffee and to watch the TV in the gulag if there was a football game on I wanted to see.

As I approached the office, I saw someone come out of the door and stalk away up the street, hunched over. It looked a little like Waters, but it was hard to see.

As I walked in, I saw Amelie at her desk, slumped a little.

'Hello,' I said. She jumped.

She didn't say the obvious 'What are you doing here?' She knew I lived close, though I'd refused her mischievous requests to come and see the place.

'Work or play?' she asked.

'Both,' I said, pretending to consider the question. I sat down and plugged in the laptop. There was silence for a while as I waited for it to power up.

'No model tonight?' she asked.

'Why do you care?' I replied. I was tired. I didn't want another conversation about Katerina. The whole situation was a little surreal, I thought. What was she doing there, anyway?

'I just don't want to see you get hurt,' she said.

I turned to inspect her. It looked like she'd been out somewhere, but the mascara was starting to run and the hairclips weren't holding all her hair properly. She looked upset and a bit drunk.

'Maybe you shouldn't worry about me getting hurt, maybe you should worry about someone else?' I suggested.

I wasn't really sure if I meant her, or Katerina.

Amelie watched me as I turned back to the laptop. I found the website and started to upload. I could have sworn her eyes were burning into me, but when I turned back to her she was walking unsteadily towards the kitchen.

'Bollocks, no coffee!' she called a few seconds later. She came back into the office. 'Dan, you got any coffee at yours?'

'We could go to a café?' I suggested. 'Put it on expenses.'

'No, they'll all be full of drunken retards this time of night. I just want to sit somewhere quiet and have a coffee and a chat with a friend.'

I really didn't feel friendly just then, but when I looked into her face, I saw she'd been crying and, as usual, I couldn't say no to a crying girl. Especially a pretty one.

'This is lovely,' she said, smirking at my room.

'Shut up, it suits me.'

'Or you suit it,' she suggested, and laughed at her own 'joke'.

I made her a coffee and we squeezed out on to the terrace. The morning was cold, but the vent from the heating duct warmed the little space sufficiently if you wore a jumper. We sat, overlooking the street still busy with hard-core clubbers looking for a new place to damage their eardrums and take their money.

I played my iPod through the laptop's speakers. The sound isn't great but it was better than the nocturnal thumps and shouts from the drunks below.

'So what's wrong,' I asked, feeling a bit as though I was starting a swim across the Channel after completing the London marathon.

'A boy,' she said.

From the laptop inside the sounds of the Futureheads' 'Danger of the Water' floated out to us.

'I didn't know there was a boy,' I replied. What I didn't say was that I thought there were lots of boys.

'There isn't. Not any more.'

'What happened?'

'You don't care,' she snapped and burned her nose on the Nescafé.

'I do care, sort of,' I said, truthfully. 'I don't care about this guy, because I doubt there's anything that special about him and I'm sure there'll be another soon enough that you'll fall in love with until he leaves you too.'

She stared at me, speechless.

'But I do care that you're upset, because I like you and I want you to be happy.'

She said nothing for a while, perhaps trying to figure out if she should be mad.

'Firstly . . .' she said eventually. 'Firstly, how do you know he dumped me?'

'I didn't think you'd be so upset if you'd dumped him.'

'Arrogant little tosser,' she spat. 'Think you know everything about women, don't you?'

I shrugged. 'OK, so tell me, who dumped who?'

'He dumped me,' she said glumly.

'He was probably all wrong for you anyway,' I said, slipping back into comforter role. How many times had I had this conversation? And always with women who weren't interested in me. Wasn't this what I'd been trying to escape when I came to London.

'He was, he's married.'

'Married?'

'Yes, and much older than me.'

My. God. Was it Waters she was talking about? Had they just had a scene at the office before I turned up?

I tried to think of a way of extracting the confirmation from her without alerting her to the fact that I already knew about her 'doing' Waters in his office.

'Is he . . .?'

. . .

'Is he . . .?'

'Yes? Is he what?'

'Does he work at the office?'

She stared at me. The dim yellow light soothed her tear-streaked features. She was wearing an old jumper of mine and I had a sudden urge to cuddle her, though whether to comfort her or myself I don't know. 'Now why would you ask that?' she said.

I shrugged. 'Just wondered if it was someone I knew, that's all.'

She was still staring at me, but she let it go. She began sobbing quietly. I knew what to do now, I'd been here before.

'Look,' I began. 'You're beautiful, you're funny. You're

smart. If that's not enough for him then he's the one with the problem. Not you.'

'Can't we talk about something else?' she snapped.

I blinked in surprise. This wasn't the usual drill. Usually this 'I'm ugly', 'no, you're beautiful' thing went on for half an hour at least.

'You said you wanted to talk about it,' I said.

'No, I said I wanted to chat with you. Not about him, just about, you know, stuff.'

'Oh,' I said. Trying to think of something we could chat about.

She didn't help. Just sat there, messy-haired in my too-big woolly jumper, looking like a bereaved sheep.

'Are you going to Paris?' I asked in desperation.

'Yes, I have to. I'm organising the models for Jane.'

We had a special deal with Jane Macauley and Waters considered her our in-house designer. She got cheap exposure on our shows, and we got first look at the designs plus exclusive interviews with her and her stable.

'I'd love to go. Any chance of me being taken along?'

'You?' she said, snorting. 'Why would they take you?'

I was a little hurt. 'Why not, they'll need someone to get the coffee, won't they?'

'Waters gets Elena to do everything. It's just about the only work she does all year. If she can keep off the sauce. They'll want you to stay here and be in the office taking calls and sending them stuff they forgot to take.'

This wasn't good news. I had been hoping to get myself

on the list. The only other option was to take a week's holiday and fly or train myself and Katerina over there separately, but it sounded like they wouldn't let me have the time off then anyway, and surely that plan was too unlikely. Even with the tickets Hans was going to send, what would I do? Everyone would be asking me what the hell I was doing there. The game would be up immediately.

No. I needed to be there legitimately.

'So Waters takes Elena, does he?'

'Of course,'

'What if she's sick?' I asked.

She thought about this. 'He might take you then I suppose, probably not James or Rashid. But why do you want to go? It's awful. It's really hard work and you don't get to see any of the events and you don't get invited to the good parties.'

'I have my reasons,' I said, cryptically, or so I thought.

'Oh, it's not her, is it? The model?'

The contempt in her voice got to me finally.

'Oh for God's sake,' I snapped. 'Don't you judge me! You're the one who's been shagging your boss.'

In my defence, I was tired. I was exhausted in fact. In a way I wanted to hurt her simply so she'd go away and I could stop thinking for a bit. Get some sleep.

'What?' she said, quietly.

'Well come on, it's not exactly a secret round the office, is it?'

She was silent a while. Then:

'Just so I know, for future reference, Dan . . .' she paused, 'which boss is it I'm supposed to be shagging?'

'What do you mean?' I said shortly, impatient with her continued denials.

'Well I have a number of bosses, and any number of people who tell me what to do. There's Melody, and Greg. Michael and Dawn and of course Waters and Jonathan at the top.'

I looked out over the orange-hued cityscape before us, chimneys as inky blots against the hazy smog behind. I was totally miserable. I wished I could take it back. A police siren went by in the street below.

'Or maybe you think I'm shagging all of them, Dan?'

'Look forget it,' I said. 'I don't care anyway.'

'Seems a strange thing to say to someone if you don't care,' she spat. Then she was up and, after an awkward period in which she tried to get herself through the narrow window, she flounced across the room and I heard the door slam.

'Bed time,' I said to myself quietly.

I checked my phone the next morning. I'd forgotten I'd been called while editing. There was a message from Rob, the delivery guy.

'Err, hi yeah, I've, err, found the *merchandise* . . .'

Oh for heaven's sake. Was he Tony Soprano?

'Please call back and let me know when I should drop it off. Evening deliveries next week should be fine.'

* * *

A few days later I was going through the post dumped in my in-tray. Elena had crept in a few minutes ago and was in Waters' office with the door closed. I was trying not to eavesdrop. I blinked in surprise when I saw there was a letter for me. I never got post. Then I saw it was from Frankfurt. The passes! I opened the envelope. There were indeed two passes inside and something else. It was an invoice from the Carlton hotel.

In the office behind I heard Waters raising his voice. 'Mumble mumble . . . mmf . . . can NOT do this in Paris! If I so MUCH as smell . . . mmf . . . mumble . . .'

There is a moment when you realise something has gone suddenly, terribly wrong somewhere, but before you quite know what, or why. You just know that it's going to be bad, and it's going to be your fault. I had this limbo-dread feeling now as I read through the document. It listed, in clinical detail, a terrible story of debauchery and destruction.

We're not just talking the sixteen bottles of extremely expensive champagne (not six, but sixteen) or the lobster meals someone had ordered from room service. But there was damage to hotel furniture as well. Broken chairs, cracked mirrors, a broken television set. One carpet had severe cigarette burns and needed to be replaced. There were other horrors as well. Porn videos, long-distance phone calls and a broken fire extinguisher.

The Germans had continued the party after we left, and

had had a pretty wild time of it. I phoned James who was at the studio.

'We only paid for the drinks for the Germans, yeah? And the meal. They paid for the room?'

'Yeah, that's the deal. The customer account pays for the room.'

I heaved a sigh of relief. I wasn't going to have to explain myself and this invoice to Adrian. Hans was just showing off.

'Oh, and extras, we pay for extras,' James said.

My heart stopped and slunk off somewhere to hide.

'Extras?' I asked tentatively.

'Yeah, you know, room service and that, we are supposed to be entertaining them.'

'Do you think damages would count as extras?'

'Damages?'

'Yeah, and porn.' I explained what had happened.

'Uh-oh. Hang on, let me think.'

I waited, chewing my nails.

'Hang on, we should be OK, you must have signed for everything when you picked up the card as we left the hotel. Only charges incurred up to that point would go on your card. Everything else will go on the customer account.'

My stomach went off to join my heart in its dark place.

'You did sign when we left, didn't you?'

'Course I did,' I said, as confidently as I could manage, lacking a heart and stomach as I was.

'Well then we're sorted, phew!' he laughed.

'Cheers, mate,' I strangled out. 'Phew!'

* * *

£10,076.

Ten thousand and seventy-six pounds.

Sterling.

The carpet cost nearly half of that, and the TV most of the rest. We could have had a few more bottles of champagne without really making much of a difference.

I knew it would be bad. I had no idea how bad. I stared at the invoice for a full minute while the attractive receptionist looked at me, holding out a pen. Her manager stood behind her. I shook my head.

But what could I do? I signed it. I'd just cost the company £10,076. Nearly my yearly salary, in one night. And what had I got in return? Two backstage passes to a crappy fashion show in Paris. Not even New York.

I took a moment, on the way back to the office, to tot up all my debts so far.

Personal overdraft – £267
Taxi rides for Katerina and friends – £60 (approx)
Loan from James – £25
Rent arrears – £335
Bill from Carlton – £10,076
Total £10,763

I'd have to make some spending cuts.

Rent was due tomorrow night. And I had a date with Katerina tomorrow. Bottles of champagne don't grow on trees. Still, no point getting despondent about it. I needed a plan. I knocked off early and went home with half a bottle of wine left over from some meeting I'd swiped from the fridge in the kitchen.

The plan was simplicity itself. There were two parts. First, I needed to avoid Ronnie tonight. By the time he came around in two weeks, I'd have been paid again and I'd have enough in my account to pay for another couple of weeks. It would leave me without any cash at all, but procrastination, or crossing bridges when I came to them, as I preferred to phrase it, was a vital part of the plan. Otherwise it wouldn't work at all.

The second part of the plan was trickier, but also more rewarding. I would gently advise Hans that I still had the footage of the debauchery at the Carlton. It might encourage him to be more realistic about whose responsibility the damage was.

'What the fuck is THIS?' Adrian screamed at me, showing me the credit card bill. He was red-faced, grey Minty-stubble thrusting out energetically.

I pointed to the Carlton bill. 'That's a mistake. The Germans are paying that.'

'Well thank God for that at least,' Adrian said, quieter now. 'What about all these other bits. Have you been having a party?'

My stomach churned, curds and whey. Was this where it

all unravelled?

'All to go on various accounts, Adrian, I have the receipts.'

That was sort of true. I had some of the receipts. But they were mostly from things I'd bought for me or Katerina, not clients or staff.

The door downstairs slammed and I leaped into action. I snapped the laptop shut and lunged across the room to the table lamp, turning it off just as I heard someone banging on a door downstairs.

Holding my breath, I crouched on the bed against the wall. I couldn't imagine Ronnie climbing on a chair to peer through the pane of glass above the door frame, but I didn't want to take any chances.

It wasn't Ronnie. It was the homeless guy from the NatWest cashpoint. He was friends with one of the drunks downstairs and came around sometimes to warm up. I exhaled with relief and sat back at the computer. I turned the monitor back on, but not the lamp, being uncertain as to whether the glow would be visible over the door. I cut, played a few seconds of Hans lunging at Rashid as they wrestled on the bed and cut the tape again. The clip was just over one meg, small enough to email. I saved it on disk ready to take into the office the next day. The door slammed again. Once more, I switched off the monitor and took up my position on the bed, ears cocked.

It was Den. The bloke from next door who worked in an 'Adult' store in Old Compton Street. He shared the room with another employee at the store.

'Shit,' I said and sat back down at the Mac. I was becoming uncomfortably aware that my bladder was full. I considered popping out quickly but thought better of it. Den and the other bloke were around, both of who would blow my cover if they saw me. Also, it would be Sod's Law if I was in the loo when Ronnie arrived. There was no way I could remain in there undetected for twenty minutes.

I tried to think of something else and willed Ronnie to get a move on.

Tonight, of course, Ronnie was late for the first time since I'd lived there. 'Regular as clockwork,' Den had assured me just after I moved in. Forty-five minutes late in fact. When the buzzer finally went off again, I almost wet myself in a Pavlovian reaction. My bladder had never been this full. All I could think of were waterfalls. To make matters worse, it had started to rain; a broken drain outside on the terrace provided an ironic water torture.

Still, nearly over, I thought. Ronnie never took longer than twenty minutes or so, even when he was arguing with one of the drunks.

Except for tonight of course. He stood talking loudly to Den outside my room for a full ten minutes discussing a blockage in the sink and then spent another good five minutes in the loo. He also checked my room twice. Knocking, then twisting the handle. I wondered what Ronnie would have done if the room had been empty but the door open. Would he have come in? Looked around?

Gone through my possessions? Stolen something?

I stood on the bed, legs clenched together and teeth gritted. Ronnie finished his security inspection and I heard the creaking on the landing. Why wasn't he going downstairs? I began to feel that Ronnie actually suspected my presence and was deliberately taking longer than necessary. Perhaps he had superhuman hearing?

Eventually I could stand it no longer. I peered around in the dark for a receptacle. Finding nothing useful, I considered the window. It would mean opening it first, I thought; Ronnie was bound to hear that. In desperation I opened the cupboard and felt inside for something I could use. My hand gripped a bottle. I pulled it out and held it up to the light shining through the pane above the door. Jack Daniel's, nearly empty. That would do. I slowly uncapped the bottle and made ready to fill it before reconsidering. The bottle was worth nearly twenty quid, full. It was precious stuff. I couldn't waste it.

The need for relief was nearly overpowering, but my need for value for money was more so. I put the neck to my lips, tilted my head back and drank the fiery liquid down in three huge gulps.

'Aaaaaah,' I said, a little too loudly, then clapped a hand over my mouth. There was another knock on the door.

Startled, I naturally lost control and only just got the bottle back into position in time. Blessed relief flooded through my tensed muscles. There is precious little on earth that can compare to the pleasant sensation of urinating after being forced to hold it in for an hour past its due date.

I capped the bottle, and settled back down. Briefly I thought of just tipping it out the window after Ronnie had gone, but decided that there were limits. I might as well cross the hall to the loo as soon as the danger had passed.

Ronnie appeared to have lost interest in my door and presently I heard the front door slam downstairs. Still quite paranoid, I held my breath and listened to the sounds coming from the rooms next to mine, for once grateful for the thin walls. Eventually, when I was satisfied that Ronnie's voice was not one of those I could hear, I quietly unlocked the door, opened it and walked out into the hall, coming face to face with Ronnie.

'All right, Maestro?' Ronnie said cheerily. His eyes flicked down to the bottle in my hand.

Lost for words, I grunted and barged on into the loo. Once inside I closed my eyes and screamed silently.

As I poured the contents of the JD bottle into the loo, I called out. 'Ronnie?'

Obviously still standing right outside the door, the landlord answered, 'Yes, Maestro?'

'Um, bit of a cash flow problem at present, err, can I fix you up next time?'

'No problemo, mate. See you then,' came the answer, followed by footsteps padding off down the hall. The footsteps stopped. 'Oh, Maestro?'

'Yes?'

'If you try this again, I'll break your nose, understand?'

I swallowed. 'Yep.'

And finally, he went.

If I were a superhero, my super-power would be the ability to look really calm when I am in fact going apeshit inside. Not much of a power, you may say, but I bet you can't do it.

I was calmer than Superman, more relaxed than Spiderman as I pressed the send button from the big Mac in the editing suite. The email read as follows:

Dear Hans,
Great party the other night, and thanks for the passes! You seem to have accidentally enclosed an invoice from the hotel in with the parcel, I'm returning it by airmail today.

Regards
Dan Lewis.

P.S. I attach a short snippet of video I found on a forgotten tape. Just for a laugh. I have others if you'd like more reminders of our great party! See you next year.

I had decided I definitely wasn't going to Paris. I'd give the tickets to Katerina and she could take a friend. I couldn't afford to fly down myself, and even if I wangled a trip via work, I'd still have to pay for her. If I just gave her the passes, she'd have to make her own way there. I phoned her to arrange a meeting-point for our date that evening.

'I have something for you,' I said.

'What is it?' She was excited, girlish.

'You'll see tonight.'

She squealed in disappointment. 'Tell me now.'

'It's something you've been wanting for a long time.'

She was silent.

'I'm not being rude,' I said hurriedly, realising she might have the wrong end of the stick.

'Look, just wait, OK? You'll like it.'

'Where shall we meet?'

'Let's just go to Starbucks,' I said. 'I'm not touching booze again for a while.' Cunning plan number twelve. We have an account at Starbucks and I can charge it all to Waters without using the card again. Also, I save money on alcohol and it makes me seem more mature.

'Have you been drinking too much while I was away?' she asked, needlessly.

'Only to drown my sorrows, I was missing you so much,' I gushed. She laughed.

'OK, see you at 7.30?'

'Sure,' I said and snapped the phone shut. Then I did that little-finger-in-the-mouth thing Dr Evil does in *Austin Powers*.

Later that day I got an email back from Hans.

Danny-boy!

Thanks for your mail. The video is so funny! I didn't know you had that! I am sorry for the invoice I sent, it is mistake and should not be on your account. Please ask my old friend Adrian to invoice us for the full amount, plus any extras you may have incurred. It was such a good night we will do it again next year and we will pay. I will make sure you have a good time, but you can do something for me. You can send me the funny tape, but not as attachment. My IT man thinks it is porn and holds up the attachment so please you send as the original tape and when I see you we have a good time, OK?

Your friend,
Hans

I smiled. The plan was going perfectly.

6

Int. Hotel room. A young blonde woman gets out of bed in a darkened room, leaving behind a figure under the covers. She goes into the bathroom and shuts the door. Cut to int. bathroom. She bends over the toilet bowl. Cut to extreme close-up of rolled up twenty pound note and line of white powder.

'So where are we going?' she asked once I'd drained my latte.

'We're going for a meal and a drink. A friend of mine works at the Carlton and he asked me to go around and check it out.'

'The Carlton again?'

'Nothing but the best,' I smiled.

We left and made our way around the corner. I held her hand as we crossed the street, no as we *floated* across the street. I could hardly believe that in a few hours, if I didn't screw things up completely, I'd be making love to this beautiful girl. It was finally going to happen.

As I walked in with Katerina, the pretty receptionist smiled at me. She may have recognised me, or she may have smiled because she smiled at everyone. But I suspected that she smiled at me because I was with Katerina. I was a guy who models wanted to be with. I was worth smiling at. I took Katerina into the bar at the back. Drinks here were expensive, but I didn't care. Someone else was paying.

This was the sort of bar where they give you posh crisps for free. We sat on a sofa that was so big and comfortable that had it met Waters' sofa in a bar it would have given it a contemptuous look. Katerina peered closely at the drinks list. Did she need glasses?

'What are you going to have?' she asked as though she'd never had a drink before. And just then I realised how young she was. She was no older than me. A child. How had she got here? Snorting coke with fat Germans and hanging about with dodgy liars in Soho hotels?

'I'm going to have a gin and tonic,' I said. Not because I liked gin and tonics, but because I couldn't remember what people drank in posh bars and it was the first safe option I could think of. 'Why don't you have a cocktail?'

She looked up at me, her eyes sparkling.

We ordered and while waiting for the drinks I pulled out the envelope containing the passes.

'Dan,' she said.

'Yes?'

'It's OK if you can't, or don't want to, get me the Paris passes.'

'Why do you say that?'

She ducked her head, staring at the table before us.

'I had a think when I was in Lincoln . . .'

'Leeds, I thought.'

'Oh yeah, it was going to be Leeds, but they changed at the last minute as usual.'

'Better light in Lincoln? More green?'

She shrugged, missing the joke, or perhaps thinking it wasn't funny. 'Dunno. Anyway, I thought I might have seemed like I was just . . . you know, using you to help me out.'

'Don't be silly, I didn't think that at all,' I lied.

'Well I just want you to know that I don't see you like that, I'm not just hoping you'll get me backstage at Paris and introduce me to loads of people. I really genuinely like you. For you.'

For some reason, this little speech discomfited me, but I wasn't really sure why. I resolved to think it over later.

'I like you too, Katerina, which is why I got you a present.' I handed her the envelope.

She squealed as she opened it and threw her slender arms around me.

'Now, this gives you access to all areas as an organiser, but you'll have to do your own schmoozing, I won't be going. You can use the other ticket for one of your friends maybe.'

She looked at me, disappointed. The waiter brought our drinks.

'Why aren't you going?' she asked.

'I have some business to take care of,' I said and clinked my glass against hers.

She sat back in the sofa and appeared as lost in thought

as she was in its voluptuous suede-ness. I surreptitiously cast my gaze up and down her long body. She wore a soft, white blouse and a brown skirt over black tights. The blouse gaped a little over her breasts and from where I was sitting, I could see a good deal of her white bra. I sat still.

Over dinner we talked about other things. She asked me about film-making and for once I didn't really have to make it up. I think I bored her because she got through a few glasses of wine while we ate the rich food. I stuffed myself, then started worrying I'd end up belching garlic fumes over her while snogging.

We finished with coffee and liqueurs, which were pretty horrible to tell the truth, but it looked impressive to order them.

I plonked the lot on the credit card. The invoice would go on the extras Hans had promised to pay. I promised myself this would be the last time I charged anything to Hans. I felt uncomfortable about doing it, but I justified it to myself for the following reasons:

1) **Dieter had virtually tried to rape Siobhan.**
2) **Hans had tried to cover it up instead of kicking his butt.**
3) **The Germans had then deliberately caused damage to the room and tried to screw me over and get me to pay.**
4) **Hans had intimated that he was prepared to pay**

for some extras, which I could interpret as being a little treat for Katerina and me.

Besides, as everyone kept telling me, everyone did it. That was just the industry. Smash and Grab, man. Hans wouldn't be personally paying for it. It would be his shareholders. Free money.

I signed the bill without looking at it. Katerina looked on, her face a mask. I smiled, nervous as an Iraqi judge.

'What now?' she asked.

'I have a room upstairs,' I said, cringing inside at how lame my seduction attempt must seem to her. I tried to remind myself just how young and innocent she had looked earlier. But that had been a thousand years ago. She held the power now. She had what I wanted.

'I'll go upstairs with you,' she said. 'On one condition.'

'What's that?' I said, a little too eagerly.

'That you come to Paris with me.'

'I . . .'

'If we sleep together, Dan,' she said quietly, 'I will be your girlfriend. You will be my boyfriend.'

I gulped. I was scared, but desperately excited. I wanted so much to be her boyfriend. I had no idea what would come next, but that didn't matter. Victory, or at least the latest victory, was in sight.

'And if you're my boyfriend, then you should be with me in Paris. Supporting me.'

I hoped she wasn't going to be one of those bunny-boiling girlfriends. That would be disappointing. I shook my head to rid it of the thought, it wasn't an unreasonable position she was taking. She was telling me I needed to be committed. To stop brushing her off when it suited me. She was telling me she took this seriously. That she was thinking further ahead than me. Not that that was saying much.

I took out my phone.

'What are you doing?' she asked.

'I'm going to ask my assistant to book some flights,' I answered coolly.

I pretended to press some buttons, hit green and held the phone up to my ear. Unfortunately I have this stupid phone that calls the last number dialled if you just hit green. Katerina's bag buzzed and she did that flappy panicky thing girls do when they're looking through their bag for their phone. I hung up.

'Oops, sorry that's me, I called you by mistake. New phone,' I explained.

She eyed it curiously – it wasn't new at all, of course. The manufacturer had gone out of business two years ago so she probably wouldn't recognise it.

What I should have done was just to pretend to press some buttons, what I actually did was press some buttons at random. Again I hit green. The restaurant was noisy so I didn't hear the phone ringing but just began speaking. 'Hi, Elena, sorry to ring so late, but I've decided I AM going to Paris after all. Could you please get me a couple of first-class tickets on the Eurostar?' I winked at Katerina. I could always pretend there weren't any available and go economy when I came to actually buy the tickets.

'Hello?' someone said in my ear. A woman's voice. 'Dan, is that you?'

Amelie.

Katerina blinked, staring at my face. 'Are you OK, you looked flushed?'

'Fine, no problem, just some . . . indigestion.' God, this was turning into a TV sitcom. More tea, vicar?

'Dan? Did you mean to call me?'

'That's right, two please,' I strangled out. I could hardly say, 'Sorry, wrong number.' Could I?

'What are you on about, Eurostar? Why are you going to Paris?'

'OK, that's fine,' I said and hung up.

Katerina was eying me oddly. The phone rang. I looked at the display, it was Amelie. Why couldn't it have been Rashid? He'd have got the message and played along. Why couldn't Amelie have a name beginning with Z?

'Work,' I said, and turned it off, back in control.

'Dan,' Katerina began.

'Yes?' My heart was slowing after the scare.

'I can't . . . we won't be able to . . .'

'Yes?'

'Aunty Mabel is staying over.'

I looked at her, smiling. What on earth was she talking about?

'Err, I mean, it's a red wing day.'

It took a minute. 'Ohh!'

She nodded.

'Well that's OK,' I said. She looked alarmed.

'No, I mean we don't have to . . . we can just cuddle,' I said, feeling like Ricky Gervais, knowing I should shut up but desperate to fill the silence. 'Or we could leave it till another time, I mean, I don't want to push you . . . I respect you too much . . . err.'

'Dan?' she said.

'Yes?'

'Shut up.'

OK, so I wasn't sleeping with her. But I was sleeping next to her, in the same bed. Or not sleeping, because I was too wound up.

We'd watched *Casablanca*, which I'd told her was one of my favourite films but I'd gone to sleep when we watched it at college because I was hung over so I couldn't remember what happened and Katerina kept asking me questions I couldn't answer.

'What's going to happen to him?'

'You'll just have to watch.'

'Are they going to end up together?'

'You'll see.'

We'd kissed, and cuddled. But there was something there, a barrier. It was a strange feeling, like we'd entered new territory without the right gear. On the one hand, knowing that it wasn't going to happen tonight took the pressure off. But it also kept some questions open. Left some tummy butterflies unpinned. Was Katerina just playing me here? Like I was I playing her? Was she really having her period? Or was that just one of those little white lies girl use to get themselves out of awkward situations. '*I like you as a friend.*'

She got up to go to the loo and I grabbed my camcorder and waited. When she came back into the room, I flicked on the light and filmed her shrieking and trying to hide her semi-nakedness. I chased her back into the bathroom and she slammed the door and refused to come out, even though I promised I'd put the camera away, which I so hadn't.

We lay against opposite sides of the door and chatted about unimportant stuff. I don't remember any of it now, it's not important. But the door helped a little, weirdly. Somehow having a real barrier made it easier just to talk. To be. Like we didn't have to make our own walls. We could be ourselves, protected as we were. I finally enticed her out again and back into bed.

'Tell me about you,' she whispered, in the dark.

'Too boring,' I answered.

'You're not *that* boring,' she answered.

I looked over at her, a dark shape in the thin light filtering through the window nets. I didn't know whether she was joking.

'I mean my life's too boring, not me,' I said, shortly.

Pause.

'Oh,' she said. Then giggled.

'What do you want to know?' I asked. Determined to show just how interesting I could be.

'I don't know, where did you go to school?'

I had this one covered, I'd already decided what to say if asked this.

'All over. My dad works . . . worked for the government. Foreign office stuff. He was always whipping me out of school and off to a new country.'

'That must have been difficult,' she said, sleepily. 'What does he do now?'

'Hmmm? My dad? He died.'

I didn't want to talk about him. But I wanted the sympathy. Her hand crept over and she gripped my thigh. She was just offering comfort, but I became aroused. Then suddenly the awfulness of what I was doing swept over me and I turned my back to her. Hiding myself from her.

She shifted and I felt her arms around my shoulders. I didn't deserve this. I didn't deserve her. I felt terrible.

But the barrier was gone.

The next day at work, Amelie tracked me down on the fire escape.

'What was all that about?'

'Oh don't,' I said. I was tired. Katerina had left early that morning, claiming she needed to be in the East End for a catalogue shoot. Things were a bit weird between us. I couldn't work out why though. We'd crossed some line last night. Something had changed, but I needed to think about what it was.

Amelie eyed me critically.

'What game are you playing, Dan?'

Smash and Grab. The game the whole world can play.

'I'm just reacting, Amelie,' I said. 'Just trying to stave off disaster.'

'I need your help with something,' she said.

'Soup?' I said.

'What?'

'Do you want me to get you some soup?'

'Soup?'

'Or water? Can I get you water? Or a tissue?'

She stared me out. 'Don't be an arse, Dan. It's your job and you wanted it.'

'Fine,' I said, ducking my head, defeated all too easily. 'What do you want me to do?'

'I need you to go to Waters' flat and find something.'

'What? What am I looking for?'

'A video,' she said.

'What's on it?'

'None of your business. Don't look at it, just give it to me.'

'Why don't you do it?' I asked.

'Because I need to stay with him to make sure he doesn't go back to his flat tonight while you're there.'

'Why don't I keep an eye on him and just phone you if he looks like going back to his flat?'

She rolled her eyes. Thought about it, then shrugged.

'I'm known there, OK? The security guard in the building would recognise me.'

I looked at her. 'What's in it for me?' Smash and Grab.

She watched me for a while. 'Do you need my help sorting out your . . . difficulties?'

'I'm not sure there's anything you can do.'

'I can get Katerina on to Jane Macauley's catwalk.'

Yes please.

So what did I do? I amended the plan. The one that had been going so well. And let's pause here and analyse this bit.

Looking back, if there was one moment where it all went wrong, one straw that broke the camel's back, one point at which I crossed the point of no return, one instant where I stopped reacting to fate and starting designing my own destruction, it was right then, when I amended the plan. When I took it a little too far. When I got greedy.

It's just that the amended plan seemed so perfect. No one would get hurt, everyone would get what they wanted. Someone else would pay.

That's the industry, yeah? Smash and Grab, yeah?

'OK,' I said, 'it's a deal.'

'Take this,' she said, giving me the key.

'This is for his flat?' I nearly asked how she'd come by it.

'No, it's for the Guggenheim Museum, I thought we could fly to New York and have a private viewing later.'

I winced. 'Sarcasm is the lowest form of wit.'

She shrugged again and disappeared back inside.

I made a call.

'Hi, Rob, Dan here. Yeah, I'm a bit tied up this week, but maybe you could deliver that stuff to me next week, Thursday? And I need you to take some of it to another address. Just one case, leave it on the doorstep, yeah? Great. See you next week.'

The new plan goes like this:

I get myself on the list to Paris, somehow. Amelie gets Katerina on to a big catwalk there; I pretend it was my influence, which it sort of was. I take Katerina out in Paris to celebrate; we have passes to all the big parties, so it wouldn't cost me anything. Katerina comes back to my hotel. The deal is sealed. I'll have to tell her the truth at some point, but that's the next phase of the plan. That happens after we get back, and I can't think about that just now. I have to sort out the money issue later too, but there was plenty of time for that.

Ring. Late in the office.

'Hi, Amelie.'

'OK, he's tied up with some things here. He'll be at least an hour, then we're going to grab a bite to eat in Chinatown.'

'What do I say if the guard asks me who I am?'

'His neighbour's name is Wilkes. Say you're a house guest there.'

'Fine.' I hung up, mouth dry.

Adrian accosted me as I was leaving.

'Did you get anywhere with that delivery?'

'Which delivery?' I replied, on guard.

'The one Karen asked you to look into. The lost booze.'

'Oh, that? No. The haulier says they never had it, the wholesaler says the haulier collected it.'

'Well did you ask for a POD?'

'A what?'

Adrian rolled his eyes. 'A proof of delivery. The wholesaler will have a document signed by the haulier proving it was collected. They will fax you a copy. If the haulier can't give you a POD to say they then delivered the goods, then they will have to pay you for them.'

'Oh.' I hadn't thought of that. I panicked that Rob and I might get caught out here, but as long as Rob didn't own up to finding and delivering the goods, which he wouldn't, it made no difference, surely.

I left the office and wandered over to Waters' building on Golden Square. A nondescript door lay open and I stormed confidently into the apparently empty foyer.

'Can I help you?' asked a security guard, popping out of nowhere. I leaped.

'Oh, you scared me,' I said, trying to remember the name of Waters' neighbour.

He nodded. 'Who are you here to see, sir?' he asked, staring at my face as if committing it to memory for the identikit.

'I'm a houseguest, with Wi-wilt?'

'Wilt?'

'Wilse.'

'Wills?'

'Wilkst.'

'Wilkes?'

'Yes.'

'OK, do you have a key?'

I held it up. He smiled. I moved on. I was good at this. I should be a spy.

Waters' apartment was a mess. And it wasn't even that big. I knew he had a house in the country where his wife and kids lived. This was just a pied-à-terre. As they called it. But on his salary surely he could afford something better?

I stuck my nose into the bedroom. The smell of unwashed sheets and the thought of seeing something disturbing in there stopped me from going further. Apart from that it was just a tiny bathroom, even tinier kitchen and the sitting room.

Behind the TV was a row of tapes and DVDs. They were neatly ordered except for one, lying on top. It had a green label. I'd seen that before. What the hell was on it? Was this definitely the one she wanted? I didn't want to have to come back. I checked my watch, still plenty of time. Amelie had asked me not to look at the tape, but how else could I be sure it was the right one? I had no idea what was supposed to be on it, but I imagined that watching it would probably answer my questions. And of course I was fantastically curious. You don't have to be a film nut to want to watch a video you've been asked to half-inch from someone's apartment.

Besides, I didn't have a video recorder at home. If I was going to have the chance to see it, it was now.

I popped it in the machine and hit play.

CCTV footage, from the building foyer looking towards the door to the office. Grainy, black and white, fixed camera angle. I watched, nothing happened. I fast-forwarded. Still nothing. I glanced at the door and checked my watch. I'd been here twenty minutes. Did I have time? I pulled out my phone and peered at the murky display. It took me a second, but then I realised what was wrong.

The phone was off.

I turned it back on, hurriedly, glancing up at the TV screen as I did so. What I saw there made me forget the phone.

Waters and Amelie were standing by the door to the office. She was against the wall. He was crowding her. Her body language suggested she didn't want him so close.

He moved to kiss her and she turned her head. His hand lifted and he held her jaw. She pushed him away and he grabbed her.

BEEP BEEP. My phone jerked in my hand and I started. I paused the tape and hit the green button. A text. From Amelie.

GET OUT NOW. ON HIS WAY BACK.

OHMYGOD! When had she sent it? I fumbled with the remote and the machine started up again. I leaped forward and hit eject, just as I saw Waters raise his hand and backhand the struggling Amelie. I flicked off the telly.

Then I heard the grinding of a key in the door. The tape machine clicked, clunked and prepared itself to open, why did these fucking things take so long? Give me CDs any day. The door opened.

I'd been in a similar situation once before. When Mum nearly caught me watching a video I'm still not old enough to watch. I'd had practice. The tape came out as the door swung open. I grabbed it and launched myself across the room into the bedroom. There I spun around looking for somewhere to hide. The wardrobe was a possibility but I had this vision of him opening it to grab some things to start packing for Paris. Instead I dropped to the floor and crawled under the bed. Just in time. I heard Waters' footsteps come into the bedroom behind me.

As I'd suspected, he opened the wardrobe and starting grabbing clothes. I could see his feet in the mirror on the far side of the bed. Then I heard his voice.

'Hi, no, I'm not coming. I'm taking a lucky lady to the Groucho. She doesn't know it yet but she's gonna have a great night.'

I didn't like the sound of this. And like a good film-maker, I reached into my jacket pocket and pulled out the camcorder. I turned it on.

'Yeah, the little bitch is going to remember this night,' he said with a vicious tone. I shuffled to my left a little. From there, reflected in the mirror, I could get a shot of his face as he stood at the wardrobe door. I zoomed in.

'Oh just a researcher. I'm going to fire her soon so I wanna have my fun first.'

I gasped, then clapped a hand over my mouth.

'No, she is good. Too good. That's one of the reasons I want to get rid of her. She wants promotion, more money. I want a cheap lickspittle, like the runner bloke, what's his name, Dan. He suits me perfectly, no ambition.

'Screw 'em,' he said. Raising his voice. It seemed who ever he was speaking to felt Waters was being a little mercenary. 'This industry lives on slave labour. They do all the work, we get all the money.' He cackled.

Then, presumably having finished, I heard his stalking footsteps leave the room, and soon after, some tapping and scraping from the sitting room. What was he doing? I hoped it wouldn't take long, because my back was killing me.

Then I heard a long, guttural snort.

Oh, *that's* what he was doing.

He didn't take long. I heard the front door slam soon after and I extricated myself from under the bed and brushed off the dust. Waters needed a new cleaner. I peered nervously around the door. It was clear. As I stepped over to the door, I passed the coffee table. There were a few specks of white powder on the glass table, and a credit card. Almost without thinking, I picked it up and pocketed it.

Then I left.

* * *

On the way back to the flat, I texted Amelie to warn her of Waters' intentions. Perhaps she was expecting them, even welcoming them. I didn't say anything about his claims that he intended to fire her, I wanted to have that conversation with her face to face.

Simon, or Stephen or Mark or whatever the homeless guy was calling himself that day, stopped in front of me to block my path on St Anne's Court.

'Spare some change?'

I regarded him. Did he recognise me? I chatted to him most days. Maybe I was different now. Different every day maybe. Not me. Not Dan. Certainly not Bryan.

I gave him 50p and walked on. I stopped at Europa and got some beers, feeling I'd earned them.

That night was rent night again. I didn't have it, again. The buzzer sounded downstairs. I wasn't going to repeat the shameful episode last time. I was determined to face up to my responsibilities. I opened the door as I heard Ronnie coming up.

'Maestro!' he called cheerfully. 'You owe me a month's rent.' I had about a quarter.

'Hi, Ronnie. Look, mate, I'm a bit short,' I said, smiling ingratiatingly. 'Can I give you what I have? And give you the rest in a fortnight?'

He continued walking up the stairs, still smiling, and walked towards me across the narrow landing.

'I'm coming into some cash soon, just waiting on a couple of invoices being paid . . .' but then I was on the carpet.

He'd hit me in the stomach, no warning. I was looking up at the dank ceiling. And suddenly my flat didn't seem so Boho. It seemed like a trap.

I couldn't breathe. Was I going to die? I told myself I must just be winded and tried to stay calm and relax the bunched muscles in my stomach.

Ronnie didn't come into the room. He left me lying there and knocked on the door of my neighbour.

'All right, Jim?'

'OK, Ronnie, here you go.'

My breath started to come back as he took the money. Then I heard him cross to my other neighbour. I sat up, not sure whether I should run for it, or slam the door shut and barricade it.

My other neighbour didn't say anything as he handed the money over, but I could see him peering into my room. Nothing he hadn't seen before. His door slammed.

I was scared.

'Maestro, I'm going down to the Crown and Two Chairmen for a pint. Come and see me within the hour with all the money.'

And then he left. He didn't need to say anything more.

I shuffled painfully over to the table and opened my wallet. The gold card stared back at me, grinning. I reached into my pocket. And there was Waters' card. I thought for a minute, my breath still short, but from the punch or from nervousness I don't know. I put Waters' card back in my pocket. Not that. Not now. I don't know what I was going to do with it, but I felt it might come in handy. I'd seen Waters' signature enough times to know I could replicate it quite easily. But I didn't have the pin, so using it would be a big deal. A one-off probably. I put the thought out of my mind, took hold of the trusty gold card and headed out into the dark Soho night.

Rob delivered the booze on Friday morning, before work. He kept looking around nervously. Presumably not as used to the seedy underworld of the media industry as I was.

'Did you make the other delivery?' I asked. He nodded.

Once it was all piled up in my room, I filmed it. Then smiled wryly and went into work.

'I don't fucking believe it!' Waters screamed, staring at me as I sat at Elena's desk opening post. 'She didn't come in?'

I shrugged.

'Did she answer her phone?'

I shook my head, sympathetically.

'She fucking PROMISED me!' he cried, grabbing his head and gurning like Pete Doherty on his third day at the Priory.

'She's off the wagon again?' Melody called from her office. 'She's our very own Lindsay Lohan.'

'That's it,' Waters said. 'She's not coming to Paris on Monday.'

'Really?' I said. 'But who's going to be your assistant?'

He stared, and smouldered, and stared again. Then he

looked around the office desperately. James and Rashid, as usual, were out on the fire escape.

'You're coming with me,' he spat.

'Me?' Trying not to grin.

'You can use Elena's ticket and hotel room.'

He walked off and I had to go outside and run down Wardour Street to keep from screaming with excitement. The plan was coming together. I tried not to think about poor old Elena.

Still, she'd got what she most wanted. A case of Scotch delivered right to her door.

Katerina was too busy with her 'preparations' to see me that weekend. I wasn't sure what her preparations might involve, but I suspected they involved laxatives, bottled water and hours on the exercise bike. We agreed to meet at the Eurostar terminal at midday on Sunday. The show started Monday.

Paris fashion week is the biggest and most expensive fashion show on the planet. Anyone who is anyone in fashion or any related industry comes here, blags as much free stuff as possible and gets wasted. Katerina and I had organiser's passes. Which effectively gave us entry anywhere in the Carousel du Louvres, which is where all the big events are held, including some of the parties. We might even be able to get into the other parties hosted by the big houses or their sponsors. We could get into any show, including backstage.

Now Katerina was on the list for Jane Macauley's show on Monday. It was make or break time for her. If she walked straight and managed to avoid grinning like an idiot, she may be noticed by one of the other houses. They'd already have her name and be curious about the new kid on the block. The whole thing seemed to be governed by whimsy and who was 'hot' at that moment. Katerina was sure she had that season's look, so the chances were reasonable that she might get another couple of shows this week and get her face into the glossies. I had a vague idea I might be able to help as well. I'd have to check out the landscape when we got there before I could be completely sure, but there was one thing I could do straight away. I made a call.

'Lucy?' I said. 'I need a favour.'

It went against the grain for me to plan too far in advance. But I'd be lying if I pretended I didn't have a lurking demon in the back of my head whispering that if Katerina did get 'discovered' and start raking in the loot, then some of that money might end up in my bank account. Or more exactly, might be used to pay off the huge debts I was accumulating.

Speaking of money, I took the rest of the Lost Booze down to Mick/Michel's restaurant. He took the lot for fifty pounds. I reckon James would have got more but I was happy with that. Plenty more where that came from – who'd notice if the odd case went astray?

I spent Saturday editing my film and made another video

diary to send back home. This time I referred to myself as a Producer.

I popped into the office to use the editing suite there, which had a VHS machine. I watched the rest of the tape. Waters hit Amelie pretty hard. After she slumped to the ground, he stormed off towards the door. As he turned, the camera got a good look at his ugly mug. He was a nasty piece of work.

I had no intention of using any of the footage I had of him against him. It was valuable in its own right. I had a vague idea about making a documentary about the seedy media underworld and the appalling treatment of juniors. Not Channel 4 material maybe, they didn't care about this kind of thing, but maybe an Internet channel, or youtube. Someone might be interested. Babylon TV, I could call it.

I finished editing what I had of the film around 2 a.m. I hadn't eaten anything except half a chocolate bar some steely-willed but naive person had popped into the fridge door at work. I'd drunk a lot of coffee and a bit of beer.

I brought it back to the flat and burned the film to CD. It was big and I left it running on my laptop while I hit the sack.

7

Morning. Grey, wet. Ext. phone booth in Gerrard St. Close-up of man's mouth speaking into phone. Soundtrack plays trance music at volume, drowning the words. Cut to exterior of booth. Man, in rear shot, hangs up and walks off. Street sweeper clears up litter from previous night.

I awoke four hours later to find an ugly and familiar face hovering over mine.

'Shit!' I cried, trying to get up. Dieter held me down. 'What the fuck?' I cried helplessly.

'Shhh,' he said. 'Stay still. We will not hurt you if you stay still. We just want the film.'

'What film?' In my confusion I thought they meant the CCTV footage of Waters, then I realised they wanted the footage of Hans.

Another voice, in German. Dieter smiled at me.

'OK, no problem, we will just take the laptop.'

'What? No, leave—'

Then Dieter punched me in the jaw, which didn't hurt as much as you'd think, but made me want to stay quiet and still for a bit.

He stood and turned to leave. I saw the other man, it was Colin. He waved. This was surreal. It was like some gangster film, but these men weren't gangsters. They were German, for a start. Are there German gangsters? Das Crew?

Colin spoke. 'Sorry about this, Dan. Hans says this is the end of it now, and we go out for nice drink next year. Say no more.' He smiled and turned to go.

I couldn't believe it. They'd just taken twelve hundred pounds' worth of electronics. That I'd have to pay for. Or find somewhere to hide the costs.

Not only that, but they'd got the disk and all the raw footage. I wasn't worried about the files on the hard disk. It was encrypted and without my password they'd struggle to get it. Hans would probably just destroy the whole computer, I told myself. The CD was the problem. That wasn't encrypted at all. If he saw that . . . well, I didn't know what would happen, but I wouldn't be able to control it. No good would come of it, that was for sure.

I sank back on the bed and held my hands before my face, willing them to take over from my shattered brain and think of something to do. I needed a new plan.

I tried to put it out of my mind by going shopping. What the hell? I figured. In for a penny now. Smash and Grab. I was up to my ears in it. Ten K for the damage to the room (Hans would never pay for it now he had the film), nearly fifteen hundred in rent and various costs, maybe a third of which I could pass on to customers. Now a twelve hundred pound laptop.

I was going to have to spend a bit in Paris, to keep Katerina happy. And I needed to look good.

I ate a huge breakfast in Selfridges café, popped upstairs to the electrical department and bought myself a flash new videophone. Then I wandered down to menswear and bought two suits, half a dozen shirts, some decent shoes and a fabulous haircut. It all went on the gold card.

I noticed a slight bruise on my jaw as I stood staring at my thin, pale self in the changing-room mirror at Topshop. My intelligent iPod must have been chatting with the in-store music system cos it was playing the soundtrack from *Pulp Fiction*. I smoothed my collar and fixed myself with a challenging glare.

As far as I could see, I told myself, I had one chance here. One shot. It all fixed around Katerina. She was my muse, my saviour and my meal ticket. It all rested lightly on her narrow shoulders like a Galliano scarf.

She had to succeed.

Katerina kissed me as I rocked up at Waterloo, looking, I admit, dashing in my suit and with a little stubble I hoped might hide the bruise. If she noticed, she didn't say.

'Ready for this?' I asked. She nodded, speechless with excitement. I smiled despite myself. She made me feel like it was all worthwhile. I was beginning to wonder if this was love. I'd never thought about someone in the way I thought about her. Respect as well as lust. But this wasn't how the songs said it should be.

Elena had been booked on an earlier train to Waters and the rest of the entourage. She (and now I) had to arrange a few things at the hotel, setting up a room for interviews and to-camera pieces. This suited me as I wouldn't have to experience any uncomfortable encounters with colleagues who might order me about and give the game away.

Thankfully Elena had booked herself a first-class ticket. I'd phoned up, changed the name and booked the seat next to it for Katerina. I hadn't needed to use the gold card for that one, I just charged it straight to Jane Macauley's account. Now Katerina was on her model list she was genuine.

On the train we sipped champagne. I ate and she pushed the food and we chatted sparingly, both engrossed in our own thoughts. As we entered the tunnel I felt a new frisson to go with all the others. This was my first trip abroad.

'Dan?' I opened my eyes. Drained from the tension of the last few days.

'Lois,' I said. It was Amelie's friend, from Mode Web. She glanced over at Katerina, snoring softly in the opposite seat . . .

I thought quickly. This was an opportunity.

'Nice to see you,' I said, standing and kissing her earlobes. 'This is Katerina, she's opening for Macauley tomorrow.'

Lois's eyes widened. Katerina opened her mouth and

sighed puffily in her sleep. She didn't look her best, I had to admit.

I'd been doing my research. Shows were opened by either huge names or new stars. Now, of course I knew there was no way Katerina was going to be opening for Macauley. Not least because Macauley hadn't even met Katerina yet. There was a real chance she might decide not to use her at all.

The thing was, this didn't matter. I just needed to get the rumour out there. OK it was a lie, but so what? Everyone gets what they want. Katerina gets the publicity, Lois gets the scoop, and the fashion world might just get a new star. I get sex.

'Is that confirmed?' Lois asked, dubious.

I tapped my nose. 'You heard it here first,' I said. 'You owe me a drink for the exclusive. Though I think there's a press release coming out.'

'Who do I call for an interview?' she asked.

'She has an agent if fashion houses want to try and book her.' I gave her Marj Newman's number. 'She also has a PR guy to call for interviews.' I gave her my new number and told her to ask for Dimitri.

'Another Russian?'

'They're everywhere, aren't they?'

'Why are you babysitting her?'

I had this one prepared too. 'I'm producing a fly-on-the-wall about young models.'

Lois smirked. 'I'll bet you are, but I thought you were ju— were a runner?'

'Was,' I said. 'I'm a producer now.'

And I meant it.

'Good for you, see you in Paris,' she said and moved off with a smile. I sat, job well done. I poured myself another glass of champagne and rubbed my sore jaw.

The receptionist at the hotel handed me a fax as I was checking in. Katerina was wandering around the lobby grinning idiotically at the chandeliers, plush sofas and liveried staff.

Dear Dan,
Here's the press release you asked me to arrange for you. As promised I won't ask questions right now but you must tell me what you're up to as soon as you get back. Better not be anything illegal is all I can say.

Say Hi to Paris from me,

Love Luce x.

The second sheet was a press release with Lucy's old PR company letterhead. I'd asked her to send it to all the usual papers, mags and websites. It read as follows:

NEW Face Katerina Roberts set to be 'the new Kate Moss'.

Until a week ago, no one even knew who she was, but Katerina Roberts, 18, from the Marj Newman agency is set to be the big discovery at this year's Paris fashion week, which starts today. Rumoured to be opening for Macauley, she's also said to be wanted by other big names including Dior, La Croix, Gaultier and D&G.

'She has the look, and she can walk,' said Roberts' PR and personal assistant Dimitri Stanislav.

The release then gave my new number and Marj Newman's details. I'd wanted to write more, but Lucy advised against it.

'Keep it short and sweet, remember, editors are lazy and desperate to fill space using as little effort as possible. Little items like that they'll just cut and paste into the page layout. If you make them actually edit by writing long tracts, they'll lose interest.'

I smiled as I read the fax and hastily hid it in my pocket as Katerina bounced up to me, grinning like Tigger on speed.

'Let's check out the room,' she said.

The hotel was fantastic. Right on the Rue de Rivoli, overlooking Les Jardins des Tuilleries. Elena had booked her own room as well as Waters'. So that was hardly surprising.

She was a woman used to the finer things in life. The only problem was we found there was no booze in the mini-bar, nor could we order any from room service. *Non*, they said. *Absolutement.*

'There must be some kind of mistake,' I said in a reasonable tone down the phone.

'Monsieur, there is no mistake, we have vair strict instructions to not take orders for alcohol for this room. This is from Monsieur Wart-hairs.'

Bloody arsing Wart-hairs.

'We could go to a bistro?' I suggested.

She looked unconvinced. 'I'm tired, I'd like a quiet night in for once. Watch some telly, chat, have a salad from room service and a glass of fizz.'

'Yeah me too. Tell you what, I'll pop out to a *marché* and grab something.'

She smiled. 'OK, I'll have a bath while you're out and slip into something more *comfortable*.'

I gulped and left quickly so she wouldn't see how red I'd gone. Was this it? Was tonight the night?

As I was out, wandering the aisles of a little supermarket in the back streets behind the hotel, it started to happen. The thing I made.

My new phone buzzed meatily in my pocket.

'Hello?'

'Dimitri?'

'Err, da?'

'This is Veronica Lacewell from BNN, could we have a comment on Katerina Roberts being asked to show for Dolce and Gabbana?'

Dolce and Gabbana?

'Err yes, she is the best new thing to happen to the fashion world since Kate Moss.'

'And is it true that Prada and YSL both want her on Tuesday?'

'Err, yes, everybody want her.'

People were watching me curiously as I wandered back and forth, looking for something demi-sec (that's what she asked for), talking into a stupidly large videophone in English with a thick Russian accent.

'How is Katerina taking this rapid ascent into the fashion stratosphere?'

Err. 'She is very focused,' I said, shrugging inwardly. A lady with a very small dog watched me with an incredulous look, as though I were Zinedine Zidane and I'd just head-butted her.

'Thank you for your time, Dimitri,' Veronica said and hung up. The phone rang again, I saw that I had two missed calls.

I grabbed two bottles of champagne and raced back to the hotel, fielding calls as I went and tripping over a very large dog crapping against a kiosk. I'd noticed all dogs in France are either tiny or huge. What's wrong with medium-sized dogs? All or nothing, Smash and Grab.

So. Everyone wanted the story. Much later I realised that

there wasn't much else to occupy fashion journalists the day before a major fashion show. Everyone was trying very hard to keep their cards close to their chest to avoid giving too much away to the opposition. Fashionistas tend to steal from each other a lot.

Through a combination of excellent timing and outrageous lies, I'd managed to make Katerina the big story.

I burst in through the door, ready to deliver my news, and realised straight away that she already knew. She was on the phone, eyes on stalks. She held her hand over the mouthpiece to call to me.

'Dan! Galliano wants me. Everyone wants me. Marj called, her phone's ringing like mad. They want me, they want me.'

Her eyes shone in triumph. And at that moment, I wanted her more than all of them put together.

We fielded calls for the next two hours. I ditched the Russian accent but had to explain to Katerina what I'd done.

'You told them you were my PR?'

'Well you needed a PR. It seemed like the best thing to do at the time.'

'That's OK, I would have asked you to do it anyway.'

'Great, is your agent miffed about it?'

'I don't think she even remembered who I was when they started calling her asking if I was free for fittings. But she did OK, she got me into Galliano, Dolce and Gabbana, Gucci and either Prada or YSL, they clash.'

'Which are you gong to do?'

'Prada of course, I'm more likely to get to keep a bag.'

'You're still doing Jane Macauley tomorrow?'

'Of course. I'm opening.'

I felt like Captain Picard from *Star Trek. Make it so.*

Her phone rang again. She took the call. I poured the fizz.

When she'd finished, she snapped the phone shut and said, 'I have to go now for a fitting for D&G. They need me tomorrow night for the show and there's no other time.'

I nodded. 'OK, shall I come?'

'Please?' she asked.

That was it for our 'quiet' evening, but I didn't mind. There would be plenty of time for us after Paris fashion week.

'Dan!' It was Waters, calling on my old phone.

'Yeah?' I looked at my watch. 3 a.m. at the Carousel. Katerina was still being fitted by a couple of dressers and a junior designer from D&G. They were tolerating my presence in an anteroom. I'd dozed a few times, wondering vaguely if Katerina had taken anything to help her stay awake. Just as well I hadn't been asleep. I would have been seriously pissed off with Waters.

'There's a model causing a storm over there, Kathy something . . .' He sounded like he'd been hitting the jazz pretty hard himself. Talking fast, garbled.

'Katerina Roberts,' I said deadpan. 'I'm with her at Dolce and Gabbana now.'

He paused. He hadn't expected me to be anywhere near the action.

'We need an interview with her tomorrow 6 a.m., can you get that?'

'No problem,' I said. 'If I can find an alarm clock.'

'I'll have a crew there at 4.30. We'll use your room, mine won't be ready. Make sure she's there, got it?'

'Yep.'

He hung up. Not even a 'well done'.

I had her back at the room just in time. She looked great. I looked awful and felt worse.

The camera crew had talked their way into my room. I stumbled in to find leads, lights and hulking cameras looming about the place, tripping me up. I grabbed a coffee and chatted to the producer while the make-up people did Katerina and Edie Morgan. His name was Stefan and he was a nice bloke. One of those people who you are sure will have loads of friends and won't have time to talk to you then makes you feel like you're the most interesting, important person in the world when you're talking to them. Good producers are like that. Good people are like that.

'You look tired,' he said.

'I haven't slept,' I replied, rubbing my jaw.

'You've got a big week coming up,' he said, sounding concerned. 'Need a pick-me-up?'

I looked up at him, startled, though it shouldn't have been a surprise. 'No thanks,' I said, wondering if I was making a mistake. But no. That way lay madness.

He shrugged. 'Have one of these then,' he said offering me a packet of Marlboro lights.

And I didn't even think twice. If I was going to pull this off, I needed something. I needed a pick-me-up *lite*.

'Sure,' I said, 'thanks,' and took a cigarette.

I looked at it. I'd tried them before of course. Who hasn't? But that was before Dad had left, before Mum started sucking like she was paid by the butt or something. I shrugged. The sooner I started the more time I'd have to give up later. I figured it was either fags or cocaine. Stefan lit my cigarette and I just, only just, managed to avoid coughing as I drew in the intoxicating smoke. I was sure he was watching me, judging me. But when I turned, he was busy adjusting the focal length on the camera. I blew out the smoke and started to feel a bit giddy.

I went to sit down and finished my coffee. My head was spinning, and not just from the cigarette. While I watched my beautiful girlfriend being interviewed by one of the UK's top interviewers I relaxed and sat back in my seat. Katerina was brilliant. She played the aloof, who-gives-a-shit starlet act beautifully. As I sat and watched the two of them seated on high chairs, the lights of early morning September Paris through the windows behind, I reappraised my own role in this. Katerina would have made it anyway, of course she would. This wasn't some piece of genius from me, nor was it the luckiest of breaks. Katerina was beautiful. One of the assistants at D&G told me 'she can walk', which apparently a lot of them can't do very well. And of course she had the look.

The interview itself was pretty dull, as it happens. Edie asked her loads of stuff about her life, most of it unknown to me. Most of it would be cut out of the final interview. I hoped Katerina and I would have some time alone after it was over. We wouldn't get much more opportunity this week. I tried not to think about kissing her, holding her, undressing her.

To take my mind off it, I hooked up my iPod. It decided to play me the *Shaft* theme. Intelligent yes. Subtle no.

After the interview I grabbed a couple of hours' sleep. Katerina didn't bother. She was high. And not on coke. She had more interviews lined up later that morning. Her agent was due in Paris later as well, and would take over the PR activity. I wasn't really needed any more and could get on with whatever Waters needed me for. I promised her I'd be at the Macauley show.

When I woke, Katerina had gone. I showered and popped down for some breakfast. Just as I was finishing my croissant, Waters showed up. He saw me, and that was the last bit of peace and quiet I had for a while.

The rest of the day passed in a whirl. I went to Macauley's show, and it was brilliant. Katerina was brilliant. She wore three outfits in all. And she looked amazing, but she suddenly didn't look like herself, or anyone I knew. She looked like all the other models. And it's strange, but I didn't really fancy her as she stalked up and down. The clothes weren't what I called flattering, and she had far too much make-up on, and pouted so much she was almost snarling.

But that was her job.

After the show, she went for more fittings and I had errands to run for Waters. The time flew and before I knew it I was alone in the hotel room around 10.30 reading a text from Katerina telling me she was having dinner with some of the other girls.

I missed her, but I knew she needed to network. I phoned Amelie instead. She came over with some beer and we ordered room service burgers and watched TV with the sound down, dubbing our own words and falling about laughing with the weirdness of it all.

It was late when I yawned and said, 'I'm hitting the sack.'

Amelie eyed me strangely. For a moment I had this weird idea that she was going to ask if she could stay. But she didn't. She kissed me on the cheek instead and grabbed her coat.

After she left, I dropped off and woke around 5.30 to find Katerina asleep next to me. I put my arm around her but she didn't wake. Exhausted, drained, like me.

I was sitting in a bar or bistro on the Rue St Honore a few buildings away from the hotel. I'd turned my phone off and was working my way through a bottle of wine and a baguette. My mind was a blur.

I had escaped from Waters by nipping out the back door of the hotel through the kitchens. He'd been holding fort in the lobby as usual, buttonholing people, name-dropping, trying to get himself on to VIP lists, chatting up models. Touching up maids. Every time I wandered into shot, he'd send me on some pointless errand. *Get me some hand wipes, buy me a newspaper, phone the office and get the ratings figures for last September, get me a coffee, get me some champagne, book me a table at the Ivy on the 13th March next year etc . . .*

I reasoned that if I wasn't visible, he wouldn't even remember I existed and the tasks would somehow become magically less urgent. I bet he didn't treat Elena like this.

I was wrong about him forgetting me though . . .

'Waters told me to come and find you,' Amelie said sliding into the booth, opposite me. She looked around at the place. It was my sort of place. High ceilings and faded glory. Scratch the gilt though and the place was teeming with woodworm.

I sighed, though in truth I was glad to see her. A friendly face. Someone normal.

'Don't worry, I'll tell him I couldn't find you. But maybe I'll spend an hour looking,' she said, reaching for the bottle and grabbing an empty glass from the next table.

'Thanks,' I said. Cramming soft, white bread into my mouth, I remembered the last time I'd sat opposite Amelie like this. She'd been doing the eating then, chicken and chips. It had only been six months ago, but it felt like a lifetime. Someone else's lifetime.

'Where's your girlfriend?' she asked, innocently. 'Did she get on any other runways?'

I smiled. 'Seriously, she and I owe you a big thanks.'

'What for?'

'For getting her into Jane's show.'

She shrugged. 'She would have got in anyway. Some of the Russians pulled out and she was a reserve, or so I was told.'

I stared at her, amazed. 'So you got me to break into Waters' flat knowing that Katerina was going to Paris anyway?'

She grinned and grabbed some bread from the basket. 'Yup, but you didn't know that at the time. You honestly believed that your intervention was necessary, and that's presumably the message Katerina got. So she thinks you did it and will be suitably grateful. Is she?'

I didn't rise to the bait. 'So like Tony Blair and the Weapons of Mass Destruction, I wasn't lying, because at the time, I didn't know I was lying?'

'Yeah, that's it! Did you get your war?'

Why was she so curious about the status of my relations with Katerina?

'None of your business,' I snapped and waved for the waiter to replace the empty bottle.

'Hah!' she laughed, rocking back in her seat and banging her head on the booth seat headrest. 'You haven't even bedded her yet.'

'Well some girls like to keep their pants on sometimes,' I said. A bit weak maybe, but I was tired.

She eyed me archly. 'Why do you have this image of me as some trollop? Is it something James said?'

I said nothing. Amelie seemed to be able to read my thoughts.

'Just because I wouldn't shag him, he thinks I must be shagging everyone else.'

Again I remained silent. I wanted to hear this.

She stopped smiling and looked down into her glass. 'He's a prick.'

'So you're not sleeping with Waters?' I asked.

'Of course not!' she cried. 'I'm not sleeping with anyone, I told you. I broke up with my boyfriend. I wasn't even sleeping with him much anyway.'

'So what about the video?'

She smiled again, her dimples crinkling. She was pretty when she smiled. Impossible to dislike.

'So you did watch it,' she said.

'Sorry,' I laughed and dropped my eyes.

'S'OK,' she replied, taking a sip of the wine. 'You were supposed to watch it.'

'What do you mean? You wanted me to see it?'

'Yes, you dope, though you don't seem to have understood why.' She wasn't catching my eye. What was she on about?

'Why? Why was I supposed to watch it?' and suddenly I thought I knew, but I didn't let myself believe it.

Do you know that feeling you get when someone you like reveals that they might just have a soft spot for you too? I'd had it maybe two or three times in my life, and one time had turned out to be a case of mixed messages. But there's no feeling quite like it. Just that quick flash in which everything is possible and before you've had the chance to think about all the reasons why not and what might go wrong. Just that brief glimpse of happiness and expectation. It's the best feeling in the world. Better than love, better than sex. Better than victory.

But it was just a flash. I clamped down on the thought and waited for Amelie to speak.

A phone rang. Amelie looked at me quizzically. It was mine. The other phone. The new phone. Dimitri's phone.

'Answer it!' she said. The moment had passed.

'Hello?'

'Dimitri?'

'Da?'

8

Ext. Paris street. Moody light and 'Ça Plan Pour Moi' *on soundtrack. Camera travels fast-mo into bistro to close-up of waiter polishing table. He looks up and smiles at the camera.*

Once again I saw almost nothing of Katerina that day. She was up and off before I stirred. Once again I spent the day running for Waters and the evening with Amelie. We gatecrashed the La Croix party and had canapé-eating contests. I commandeered trays-full by waving my pass at the waiters.

I did hook up with Katerina for a short time at a reception thrown by the organisers. She was being introduced around by her agent though and I could hardly get a word in. She did find the time to tell me she'd be off with her new model friends again that night.

'I'm sorry, Dan,' she said in response to my hangdog expression. 'It's important that I network here, I might not have another chance.'

I nodded, I did understand, but I had this awful feeling something was being taken away from me. I was losing something.

'I'll see you tomorrow,' she said and was dragged away by Marj.

I woke again at 5.30 a.m. the next morning. This time there was no Katerina. Just a text saying she'd got wasted and was staying in another model's apartment on the other side of the city.

Katerina was showing for Galliano the next day, the Wednesday. 4.30 p.m. That was the last show for the day, the stopper. After that everyone would be off to their parties. I hoped to catch up with Katerina at the Galliano bash. I was counting on my organiser's pass to get me in. I'd had a couple of texts from her that morning, but I could tell she was really busy.

Then she phoned me.

'Hi, you,' she said.

'You've forgotten my name,' I accused.

'No, Don. I haven't,' she said.

'How's things?'

'Great, but I'm missing you,' she said.

'I'm missing you too.'

'I'm really sorry I haven't been around for you, Dan, after all you've done.'

'Don't be silly,' I said softly. 'This is what you've been working for. There'll be plenty of time for . . . us when we get back to London.'

'I'm really looking forward to that,' she said. 'Maybe I can finally get to see your flat!'

I laughed. No fear.

'Oops,' she said. 'Gotta go.'

I felt much better after the call. I just needed to be patient.

Perhaps it was just as well she was so busy. I had my own work to get on with and I didn't want her hanging about while Waters ordered me around. The camera crew Waters had put together was the most inept group of individuals on the planet. They'd forgotten EVERYTHING. They'd even brought the wrong camera. I spent most of the afternoon shuttling back and forth between the hotel and the Carousel. Edie Morgan was wandering about with her own, smaller crew and they needed regular cups of tea and little parcels brought to them from the hotel.

Finally they were pretty much finished and I went backstage with my camcorder. They wouldn't let me into the dressing rooms, but there was plenty to see. My cover story was that I was making a documentary but no one seemed bothered by my presence. Everyone had something to do and fast. There were racks of clothes being pushed around. People wearing headsets, shouting, couriers delivering things or taking things away. I got some great footage, including a brief shot of Galliano himself standing in an empty room, looking a little forlorn.

I texted Katerina and she popped out briefly, not wearing very much and making me go a bit funny. She kissed me. 'Where are you going to sit?'

'We're standing, at the back.'

'We?'

'Me and Amelie.'

'Uh-huh,' she nodded and looked away, waving at someone. 'I'll look out for you, gotta go. See you at the party!' and she disappeared again. I smiled, staying positive.

Back at the hotel after the show, my work phone rang.

'Hello?'

'Dan?'

'Yes?'

'It's Adrian.'

Shit, what did he want? Dumb question, I knew exactly what he wanted. I'd dumped a pile of receipts and purchase orders on his desk before I left. I'd done so in the vain hope that he might be able to marry them somehow to the charges on the credit card bill and magic away the rest. The big Carlton Hotel bill I was thinking I'd simply blame on Hans and get James and Rashid to back me up.

As for the more recent purchases, they wouldn't be showing up yet. They'd be dealt with in the next phase of the plan.

'Dan, these receipts don't cover half of the expenses you've run up.'

'I thought there was an amount just written off as miscellaneous.'

'Only three hundred a month, Dan,' he fired back, exasperated. 'You've got thirteen hundred unaccounted for here.'

Wow, was it really that much? He went on.

'And you told me to charge the hotel damages bill to the German account, but they're rejecting it.'

'What? Why?' I blustered but I'd known this would be the case. I had nothing on Hans now.

'They say it was the cost of a party in their room which you organised.'

'That's ridiculous, those bastards!'

'They're the clients, Dan. In cases like this we have to take the hit. Did you cause this damage?'

'Of course not, they did it after we left. Ask Rashid or James.'

'So why was your card still open?'

I paused.

'Did you forget it?' he asked.

'Look, Adrian—' but he cut me off.

'Dan! This is damn close to embezzlement. This bill needs to be paid. I'm going to have to talk to the directors about this . . .'

'Sorry, Adrian, gotta go, Waters needs me!' I called and hung up.

I sat there for a while, in the empty hotel room, head in hands. Then I leaped up, grabbed a cigarette and a bottle of champagne and headed for the bath. I needed to get ready for the Galliano party.

'Wow!'

That was all I could say for the first few minutes. Amelie

had been before and was playing it cool, but she was pretty gobsmacked too. Now I don't know that much about fashion, but even I recognised a lot of the people there, and there were some big names. There was also a lot of very expensive food, which no one seemed to be touching, and even larger quantities of champagne, which everyone was downing by the bucket.

The room itself was amazing. Huge chandeliers bigger than my bedsit drew the eye up to the soaring ceilings. Your feet sank into the soft red plush and there were more flowers than when Diana died.

'This looks like a great party,' I said, lamely.

'Come on,' Amelie said. 'Let's get drunk.'

There were all sorts of people there. Film stars, rock stars. Not the huge ones of course, but some biggies. There were people from the fashion world whose names I knew but who I wouldn't have recognised without Amelie's help.

I found Katerina after half an hour of wandering about with Amelie, grabbing flutes and downing them. She was talking to a man who had his back to me.

'Katerina!' I cried walking up. She looked and smiled. The man turned to look as well.

It was Hans.

'Dan,' he roared and picked me up in his trademark bear hug. I dropped my champagne glass in surprise. Amelie looked on in alarm.

'You're here,' I said, as neutrally as I could manage after he'd dropped me with a thud on the shag pile.

'Yes, I come and stay in this hotel every year. Always the same suite.'

His eyes dropped to my badge and he smirked.

'I'm just telling Katerina here she should come and work for me. Very big show in Germany. I get her a good part.'

I raised an eyebrow at Katerina; she shrugged and smiled.

'I bet you'd like to give her a big part,' Amelie said sweetly.

'Yes. I give her a HUGE part,' the blond German roared.

I grabbed another glass from a passing waiter. Here I was, standing two feet away from the man who'd landed me with a ten thousand pound hotel bill, stolen my laptop, had me beaten up and was now trying to shag my girlfriend. I was a little jumpy, but determined not to let him see.

'And what about you, Dan?' he went on. 'You are a little film-maker, no?'

'No, I've finished with film,' I said, playing the game out. I fixed him with a stare. My British POW to his camp commandant. 'I lost my computer.'

And then I saw it. A slight flicker of his eyes upwards. Towards the rooms. He had the computer here.

'Good,' he said, 'there are better things to do. Like parties and drinking and sex.' And with that he leered at the girls. I'd had enough.

'Do you mind if I borrow Katerina for a moment, Hans?' I asked. He shook his head and turned to Amelie, who shot me a murderous glare as I escorted Katerina away.

'Having a good time?' I asked sarcastically.

'Yes,' she replied, missing it. 'I'm making so many contacts . . .' and as if to illustrate her point a photographer appeared from nowhere and snapped a few shots. Some overdressed bird poked her nose in straight after and said, 'Great show today, Katerina, my people will be in touch about New York, OK?'

She nodded, smiling, then did her waving-at-someone-across-the-room trick again.

'I have something I need to do,' I said. 'Can we meet later?'

She wasn't listening, just staring around the room, glassy-eyed, smiling and waving. I stood still and watched her. She'd arrived. It had happened for her.

And it was obvious what was happening here.

She didn't really need me any more. Maybe she never had. I was just a runner, after all. It was no more than I deserved, for my lies and manipulations. She'd played the game better than I.

'What was that?' she said finally and looked at me. I stared back, coolly. Suddenly I was angry. I was tired and I was grumpy. I lost it. I'd worked hard for this too. Where was my reward? Where was my cut? She needed to fulfil her side of the deal. Smash and Grab.

'Will I see you later?' I repeated a little harshly.

'Yes, of course,' she said absently, her eyes flickering around the room. 'I'll probably stay here, though some of the other girls were talking about going to a club. Text me.'

'OK,' I said, still staring at her and trying to calm down.

I took a deep breath. After all, the new plan was starting to take shape. I had some vague idea about getting into Hans' room and pinching the laptop back, or the disk at least. I wasn't sure exactly how, but once I'd done that I could catch up with Katerina then get her back to the hotel room. Tonight was definitely the night. If I didn't make my move tonight, press home the advantage, engage the enemy, then I might never get another chance.

It was all or nothing.

It immediately went tits up.

This is how it all came undone.

I went to the loo to splash some water in my tired, staring face, then returned to where Hans was standing. I had to rescue Amelie who was still glaring at me. Then from stage left I saw Waters stalking towards me, looking equally furious. He obviously had some fantastically important job for me, like getting his shoes cleaned. Or buying him a new tie. I considered escaping and even glanced around quickly. Then I saw something to make me panic, through a gap in the partygoers. It was Katerina, she was talking to Lois. As I watched, she turned to me and pointed, then the two of them walked towards me. Lois waved and smiled.

I looked back at Waters. The crowds had parted for him too. Twin corridors of disaster had opened. Where they met, the node of calamity, was where I stood.

It must have been like this for the lookout guy on the *Titanic*. Up there, isolated in his crow's-nest, almost separate from the scene. Watching the iceberg and the ship close inexorably. Knowing what was going to happen, knowing the broader ramifications, yet utterly powerless to prevent it.

The three of them reached me together. Hans and Amelie looked on.

'Where the fuck have you been?' was his opening gambit.

'Err, I was looking for you,' I replied limply. I could feel four sets of eyes burning into me from either side.

'Right!' spat Waters. 'I've got a list of jobs for you as long as my arm. See if you can get them done competently and then I'll think about not firing you. First get up to my room, call Kushner and arrange a lunch for us tomorrow somewhere local. Grab my brown shoes and get them cleaned, then phone Adrian in London. He was on at me before about some invoices which need clearing up, and a hotel bill?'

I blanched. Still refusing to look at Katerina, I said nothing. People around us had stopped talking and were openly listening to the exchange. Waters was enjoying the audience.

'And keep your phone on this time, you little shit,' he finished, venomously, and turned to go.

It was an exercise in power. The jobs themselves weren't important. The concierge would have had them done quicker and better than I could. Waters was pissed off at me for not being available. Not being there to kick around in front of other people.

'Who the hell is he?' Katerina asked. I forced myself to

look at her. 'That's my boss,' I said. I felt sick.

'Why is he ordering you around like that?'

I said nothing. The bullshit reserves were empty.

Lois piped up not very helpfully, 'Don't you have runners to do that kind of thing?'

Then Amelie spoke up. 'Dan used to be a runner. Waters must have been confused, he's drunk, or stoned. Dan was promoted months ago.'

I turned to look at her. I was astonished. Why was she helping me? Katerina looked at her, bemused; Lois was outright suspicious.

It was a brave stab, and I was touched by the gesture, but it was never going to wash. It was time to come clean. I didn't have the energy any more.

'No, Waters isn't confused, I am just a runner.'

Katerina stared at me, dazed. 'What? But you said . . .'

'I know, I told you I was a producer. I wanted to impress you. I'm sorry. It just got out of control. I wanted to . . . to help you.'

Hans exploded with laughter. Amelie looked awkward. Lois raised an eyebrow and glanced at me wryly. Katerina just stared. 'So how did you get the tickets?' she asked, stroking the label stuck to her Prada handbag.

'Hans got them for me.' There was little point going into the details of that little exchange just now.

'How did you get me on to Jane Macauley's catwalk?'

'I did that,' Amelie blurted out. 'Dan asked me to and

I pulled some strings. But it wouldn't have happened without Dan.'

Hans was still laughing.

'Ohh, Danny-boy,' he said. 'You are one piece of work. I love this guy,' he snorted, putting one arm around Amelie, who shivered it away. I could sense the people around us still listening in. Eager for some early dirt on the new girl.

I hated him. I turned to Katerina. 'Can we go somewhere quiet to talk about this?'

Still stunned, she let herself be led away. Amelie and Lois followed. Hans shouted after.

'Room number 448, girls, if you are looking for a real man!' he hooted with derision and was swallowed up in the crowd.

Imagine a cockroach, which'd been scuttling around a dark kitchen for months, happily eating whatever it wanted, leaving its filthy footprints everywhere. Then imagine that someone had come in and flicked on a light, with the cockroach caught square in the middle of the floor. That's how I felt just then, like that cockroach. My iPod would have played 'Nowhere to Run, Baby, Nowhere to Hide'.

But at least cockroaches lack the brains or the eyesight to see themselves as they really are. It wasn't just that a light was shining on my lies. It was that I'd suddenly been handed a mirror at the same time.

We sat in the bar at a small table.

'Where did you get all the money from?' she asked. 'You

can't have afforded hotel rooms and champagne on a runner's salary.'

'No,' I said, and coughed. 'I suppose I'd better tell you the whole story.'

I did so, even the bits with Hans and the hotel room bill and the stolen laptop. She stared, agog. I was dimly aware of Lois and Amelie standing behind us, like boxers' seconds ready to throw in the towel. I tried to put out of my mind the fact that Lois was a journalist who may decide to splash this story across the fashion press the next day: 'New Face of Paris Katerina's Slimeball Boyfriend'. I had to hope Amelie would induce her to sit on the story instead.

'You lied to me, Dan,' she said quietly.

'I did,' I agreed. 'It was before I knew you.' How limp was that?

'And when you got to know me better? When we slept together? Did you not think about telling me the truth?'

I was about to say, 'Of course I did . . .' But it struck me then. I hadn't. I'd never considered telling Katerina the truth. It just wasn't something that had ever crossed my selfish, narrow little mind. All I wanted had been to get into her pants.

'You expect me to forgive you?' she asked, reading my thoughts as per usual. I didn't pause.

'No,' I said, shaking my head. 'I don't expect you could.'

'What are you doing, Dan?' she asked, desperate to understand. 'Why did you do this? Do you think this is some kind of game?'

I wanted to tell her I knew it wasn't. But I knew that

I'd been acting as though I were playing. Playing a game that wasn't.

I was utterly defeated. There was no coming back from this, I knew.

Katerina stood suddenly, not looking at me. 'I've got to go,' she said and ran for the door.

I made to move after her. 'Let her go, Dan,' Lois said. 'I'll go after her and make sure she's OK, but I think she needs to be away from you for a while.'

I looked at her. We both knew a while meant two to three hundred years. Lois left, sliding between guests.

'Dan,' said a voice from behind me.

'Yes, Amelie,' I replied.

'Was there any footage on your laptop that might be important to anyone else? Say me, for example?'

Shit. This was the last thing I needed.

'Yes, Amelie. I'm afraid there was.'

'Oh for Christ's sake, Dan!'

I felt like a geek schoolboy, caught picking his nose, being jeered at by the cool girls.

'The laptop is encrypted, he won't be able to look at the files . . . except . . .'

'Except what?'

I told her about the disk left in the D drive.

'Great, so now scandalous images of various high-profile people in the fashion world are going to be doing the rounds of the fashion websites and I'm going to get blamed for it,' Amelie said.

'Why will you get the blame?' I asked, not really thinking straight. She smacked me gently on the forehead.

'Because I'm the only one who knew about the tape, and I'm the only one with a key to Waters' apartment.'

'Oh yeah.'

'We've got to get the disk back,' she said.

Just at that moment, I didn't want to do anything less. I shrugged.

'Does it really matter?' I asked. 'Who cares if Waters is exposed as a thug? Who gives a shit about Jane Macauley's coke habit? Or Edie Morgan taking a piss on her own lawn?'

Amelie tutted. 'They might be blackmailed, Dan. I'll be fired. Edie doesn't need this kind of publicity. And what about the shots of Katerina in her undies? Do you think she wants those on every sleazy website?'

Maybe she did, I thought, uncharitably. Any publicity and all that, but I could see Amelie had a point. Those were my images, if anyone was going to use them it would be me.

'Besides,' she said, 'don't you want to screw Hans over? You can get him to pay his bill at least if you have the pictures.'

That clinched it.

'OK,' I said, 'let's do it.' I focused on how much I hated Hans.

'Oh, but you need to get Waters' shoes cleaned first, OK?'

I glared at her.

'Only joking,' she said. 'Mr Touchy.'

We had a stiffening drink, then headed up to Waters' room. I grabbed a suit and went back down to reception.

'I'm Hans Richter's assistant, he's in room 448. I need to drop off this suit and collect some items for him, but he forgot to give me the room key.'

The receptionist looked a bit unsure, but she saw my pass and gave me the key.

'Please return it before you leave,' she said. I nodded.

Then upstairs to Hans' room where Amelie was waiting, trying not to grin.

'This isn't a game,' I hissed, echoing Katerina.

'I know,' she hissed back, trying not to smirk.

We went in and I saw the laptop immediately. It was in pieces on the desk. I heaved a sigh of relief. He obviously hadn't been able to get it working. Getting the CD out was more difficult. The laptop wasn't working so I couldn't just hit eject. Instead I grabbed a letter opener from the draw and tried to prise it open. Amelie was poking through Hans' cupboard as I did so.

Then I froze as we heard a card swipe through the door lock and the beep of the door acknowledging it. I turned to look at Amelie. She indicated the cupboard and dived inside just as the door opened. I had a better idea. Remembering Hans had told us he had a suite of rooms, I tried the door connecting to the next room, it opened and I shot through.

I had to think. Amelie was trapped in Hans' room. I still didn't have the CD. What to do? I didn't want to leave the room because I might not be able to get back in. I couldn't go back in through Hans' door now. Why hadn't I just taken the damn laptop? I'd also left Waters' suit in the room. I wasn't covering myself in glory here.

I hid in the cupboard in the dark room and tried to think up a new plan. Then my phone buzzed with a text. It was Amelie.

OOPS! WHER U?

IN NXT ROOM.

DAM, ME SO DUM!

WOTS HPPNG?

HANS GOT GIRL, CHAMPERS AND COKE!

CAN YOU SEE THEM?

A pause

CAN NOW, OPENED DOOR. BAD NEWS.

WOT?

GIRL IS KATERINA.

I sat there in the cupboard of someone else's hotel room in Paris, trying to make sense of this latest piece of awfulness. Katerina with Hans? We'd been here. We'd sorted this. She wasn't interested in him. She didn't need his crappy TV shows. Was it the coke she was after? Was she going to sleep with him? Was she doing it because she was angry with me? Or would she have done it anyway? All I knew is that I felt lower at that moment than I have ever felt, before or after.

Then the cupboard door opened and I nearly wet myself. That wouldn't have helped.

But it was only Amelie.

'Hello,' she whispered, cheerily. She was enjoying this. 'They went into the bathroom.'

'For some charlie?' I asked.

'Maybe, though Hans was running the bath,' she replied, her face unreadable in the darkness.

'Come on,' I said. 'I've had enough of this, sod the CD, let's go and get drunk.'

'Are you OK?' she asked, her voice suddenly serious and grown up.

'I will be,' I replied. 'I'm eighteen years old, I'm in Paris with free booze and a beautiful girl, how can I not be OK?'

'Great,' said Amelie. 'I'm thirsty.'

I wished, just once, that my insides could be as calm as my outsides. I stood and we left the room, heading back to the party.

There weren't enough canapés, we discovered, so we went out to dinner. I asked the guy on the door to recommend a really great place. It was just as you'd expect an expensive Parisian restaurant to be. Velvet drapes, plush carpet, loads of small tables. Sour-faced waiters. Amelie was drunk by now so she didn't feel intimidated, but I was a bit nervous. Still, I knew what to do. I'd seen this in a movie.

Lord knows what they thought of two teenagers wandering in at 10.30 p.m. If they had a problem with it, they didn't show it. Probably used to young, drunk fashionistas this time of year. Probably figured I'd have a company gold card.

I asked the waiter to recommend something. Then I asked the sommelier to recommend a wine to go with it. Easy.

Well, it's easy when you have money. I couldn't help but notice that the wine list didn't have any prices. If you have to ask . . .

'Who's paying for this?' Amelie hissed at me, trying to whisper but actually ensuring that everyone in the restaurant could hear.

'It's on me,' I replied hurriedly.

She frowned. 'You can't afford this.'

I smiled back at her.

'No,' she said. 'You can't charge this to the company. Not now.'

'I'm not,' I said. 'I'm charging it to Waters.'

Then I pulled out his credit card and dropped it on the table. It still had tiny grains of coke attached to it.

Amelie thought for a bit. 'Let's have dessert too.'

'*Naturellement*,' I replied.

'Did you mean what you said before?'

'What was that?'

'About me being beautiful?'

I had to think back, then I remembered. In the cupboard.

'Yes, of course. You are beautiful.'

A pause.

'Do you fancy me, then?'

I can't quite remember how we came to be in this position. Back in the hotel room. My hotel room, Katerina's hotel room, Elena's hotel room.

Amelie lay with her head in the crook of my arm. I held a glass of Scotch and dry on my chest. The ice clinked and made beautiful music. The party was still going strong downstairs and we'd popped back for a while after the meal but with full stomachs and fluffy heads, we'd grown tired of the heat and the jostling from overexcited queens. I remember Amelie grabbing my hand and pulling me out through the main doors, but nothing else until this. I was very drunk. Amelie must have been as well to judge by the quantities she'd consumed.

I was tired of telling lies.

'Yes, I fancy you.'

'Then kiss me.'

So I did. I was single. I was in Paris. What would you have done? Her lips were soft, oh so soft. Her breath was champagne sweet. She was warm and huggable. Being with her helped me forget my problems, both immediate and longer-term. Save me, Amelie.

She shifted and suddenly she was on top of me. She felt less bony than Katerina, more pliable. More pliant. She wriggled on me and we kissed more passionately. My hands slid down her hips.

And then there was a light shining from the doorway. And a figure standing there at the foot of the bed, shadowed, and though I was drunk and swooning, and half-asleep to tell the truth, I knew that it was Katerina. Fresh agonies, new humiliation. What more?

'I see,' she said. 'I can't say I'm too surprised.'

I sat up. Amelie slid off the bed and disappeared.

Attack being the best form of defence, I asked, 'How was Hans?'

She paused before responding. 'Is that what this is? Revenge?'

I shrugged. 'You're finished with me, aren't you? You were never interested in me, not in that way.'

I heard her gasp. I'd shocked her. Good.

'So now *I'm* the liar?'

I dimly noticed Amelie slipping out the door. Katerina didn't acknowledge her at all.

'Well now you come to mention it, yeah!' I snapped, standing up. I didn't want her having all the high ground. 'This is a two-way street, Katerina. You wanted something from me, I gave it to you, you promised me something in return.'

I didn't really mean it to come out that way, but looking back now, that was pretty much exactly what I felt.

Awful, isn't it?

She was silent for a while, then I realised why. She was crying.

'I'm sorry,' I said, belatedly remembering she wasn't some character from a film. She was Katerina.

'That's all this was for you?' she asked, her voice thick

with ruptured regard. 'You just wanted, what, sex? A trophy girlfriend?'

I said nothing, I'd kind of overstated my position as it was.

'I thought . . .' Again she paused.

'What?' I asked softly.

'I thought you loved me.'

I sort of did. But I couldn't say that, could I? You can't say 'I sort of love you'. The problem was that I didn't fully understand what I felt for her. I wanted to be with her. I wanted her around. I wanted to get to know her better. Maybe it would have led to love. But I wasn't going to lie about it. Fine time to discover honesty, you might think.

'I . . . I'm not sure,' I said, pathetically.

'I thought I loved you too.'

I hadn't expected her to say that. My legs felt suddenly weak. Why couldn't I get my shit together? What was I doing?

Then I remembered about Hans and tried to reassemble my mutinous forces of justification.

'But what about our German friend, then? It didn't take you long to get over your feelings and hop into bed with him.'

Her face flicked up towards me and I caught a flash of anger in her large, inaccessible eyes.

'You . . . arse!' she spat. 'I wasn't there to sleep with him!'

'Then why? For some charlie?' I retorted, determined to hang on to my last shred of justification for what was, let's face it, some pretty appalling behaviour. She was rummaging in her handbag, and before she pulled the CD out it hit me, hard. She threw it down at my feet.

'I was there for that, Dan. I thought you could use some help. Now I see that you were just helping yourself, as usual.'

There wasn't anything else to say. I was pretty much done. I sat on the bed and tried not to cry.

'What are you going to do now?' she asked eventually.

I knew the answer to that one at least. 'I've got to get back to London, sort my mess out.'

She nodded. She looked so beautiful standing there in the slanting light from the hallway. If only I'd played it better, I could be taking her in my arms now, pulling her gently down on to the bed, on top of me.

But maybe this was better. Maybe this was what I deserved. I shouldn't be rewarded for lies, for theft. Katerina deserved better than a cheat. I stood and grabbed my bag, shoved my few possessions into it, including the CD, and stood before Katerina.

'Despite everything, despite all the lies I told, and all the rotten things I've done, you were the best thing that ever happened to me,' I said softly. 'And I don't regret that at all.'

She said nothing, wouldn't even look at me.

And then I had to go.

9

Helicopter shot of Eurostar travelling towards tunnel from French side. Cut to int. Close-up of Dan, face pale and drawn. He wears sunglasses. His face is a mask. Internal dialogue begins.

Trains have an inexorable quality about them, a sense of momentum. Once in motion they don't stop easily. Every second brought me closer to London, the world I'd briefly escaped. The land I'd soiled and despoiled. I had some cleaning up to do.

In a way I was looking forward to it. I had no one to blame for the events of the past few months other than myself. I'd been punished, partially at least, by having my prize withdrawn. My reward put beyond reach. Had I achieved the reward it would have made no difference though, I understood that now. I needed to make amends. Fix what I'd broken. If I was able to do that, I might be able to look Katerina in the face again. Or Amelie for that matter.

Things had got out of control over the last few months. And moving to London wasn't supposed to be about losing control, it was the opposite. Taking responsibility for my actions was a way of taking control back. It was a way of forcing myself to grow up.

I knew exactly what I was going to do. Entering that tunnel was the first step. Once inside there was no withdrawal.

I went straight to the office when I got back to Waterloo. It was past midnight. No one was there of course, at that time on a Friday. I had the editing suite to myself, and I used it.

I found a few sweet tracks on unsigned.com and set about making my confessional. I used the rough shape I'd been working on for the documentary I'd been planning and I put everything on there though with faces pixellated. Amelie's legs, my flat, my payslip, Waters shouting at James, Jane Macauley snorting coke, stolen booze, Waters hitting Amelie, Katerina in her underwear, Hans grabbing Rashid, Amelie slumped at her desk at three in the morning, Edie Morgan urinating in her garden. Then I took the sound down and had Waters' disguised voice explaining exactly how contemptuously he viewed juniors in general, and Amelie in particular.

Throughout, I provided a running commentary:

'This is the flat I rented. I soon found I couldn't keep up the payments. The landlord beat me up so I took money from the company to pay the landlord.'

'This is one of my colleagues, she works fourteen hours

most days and last year had a pay rise less than inflation.'

'This is the hotel room I blagged in Paris by sending a case of Scotch to the alcoholic who was supposed to be staying here.'

'This is my boss. He's a thug and plays solitaire most of the day.'

'This is the girl I lied to most of all.'

It would be pretty obvious to the main players who they were. But not to those outside the industry, or even the company really. I didn't want to start any lawsuits. I didn't want anyone to feel blackmailed. I wasn't playing those games any more. The purpose of the video was to land myself in the shit. Not anyone else. But I also wanted to give some background, to show some of the danger in chucking young adults into a world of glamour, parties and high living without showing them the ropes properly. I wasn't trying to blame someone else, but I wanted everyone to know about the pressures I'd faced. I wasn't pure evil. There were *circumstances.*

I prepared a brief statement that I filmed myself reading and added to the beginning of the movie – this is how it read:

Hi Guys,

First of all, sorry. I've done a few things I shouldn't have and some of you are going to have to spend a bit of time, effort and money sorting it out. I've enjoyed my time here, mostly, and I've prepared a short video of the highlights of the last few months. Identities have been masked to

protect the innocent. Thanks for the free stuff and James, I promise I'll pay you back that pony before anything else. I'm going home now to see my mum and wait for the police to come.
Cheers

And that was that. I checked it over one last time, and emailed it to everyone in the office.

I went home to grab a few things from my flat. I checked the fridge. One last bottle of champagne awaited me. I squeezed myself out on to the terrace one last time and drank the fizz from a plastic cup I'd hastily washed out.

A manky, club-footed pigeon eyed me suspiciously as I gazed out over the rooftops. Now the video was done and sent, I felt more settled. The champagne helped too. It was late afternoon. I'd been in the editing suite for fifteen hours and my back ached. I set up the video camera and toasted myself for a job completed, if not well done.

Then I left for the last time and made my way down Wardour Street towards Waterloo. I passed Steve, or Dave, the homeless guy, on my way.

'All right, mate,' he said, 'spare some change?'

I pulled out my wallet and peered inside. I still had the fifty pounds Mick/Michel had given me. I needed ten pounds for my train fare and a coffee. The rest of it I didn't want. It was tainted. I gave Steve/Dave the two twenties. He smiled, showing me all three of his teeth.

'Thanks, mate,' he said. If it had been a cartoon, beer

cans would have appeared in his eyes.

'Spend it wisely, Steve,' I said and walked on.

Epilogue

Ext. Sequences of shots showing empty streets in a drab town. Cut to established shot of Dan's house. Cut to Dan in his room, staring out of the window and smoking.

And that was that, or it should have been. If those damn women hadn't screwed it all up again. Two of them. One old and one new. This is what happened next.

Mum didn't seem too surprised to see me when I walked back through the door. She didn't seem to mind me being back though, even when I started bumming her fags. That first night I was back, my sister was out with her mates and Mum and I sat side by side on the sofa watching Noel Edmonds and smoking Lucky Strikes. Amelie phoned a few times, then stopped when I didn't call back. I felt bad about that. I missed her. But I was in no fit state to be seeing anyone, and she just reminded me of a time that was now over.

A few mornings later I was in bed, which is where you first found me, worrying about debt collectors and cops. When the doorbell went I thought, 'That's it.' But I didn't get up. I lay there, staring at the ceiling until the door opened.

'Go on in,' my mum said, and coughed.

Katerina entered. I sat up straight, suddenly achingly aware of my pop star posters and unwashed pants on the floor.

She stood awkwardly and smiled, taking in the ghastliness of my lower-middle-class bedroom.

'Not quite Paris,' I croaked, worrying that she might be able to smell my foul breath from where she stood near the door, as if imagining she might need to make a break for it.

'At least it's real,' she said, and came over to sit at the end of my bed. 'Can we talk?' she said.

'Can I get dressed?' I asked.

We went down by the canal, the only vaguely nice place for a walk and a chat. I hoped the kids from the nearby council estate wouldn't be down there hurling shopping trolleys at the heron again.

She'd come to tell me two surprising things, it turned out.

The first thing she said took the wind out of my sails.

'I've taken care of your debts,' she said.

My mind twisted. Relief collided with annoyance and pride.

'You shouldn't have done that,' I said, a little ungratefully, perhaps.

'I've got the money now, thanks to you.'

'It wasn't thanks to me, you would have made it anyway. I probably held you back.'

'Don't be silly,' she said, but didn't argue further.

'No, it's my responsibility, that debt.'

'Don't be all male. I can earn that in a day. Anyway, it's done now.'

She didn't understand. I needed the debt. I needed the guilt, the worry. I needed to face up to the consequences of what I'd done.

But I hadn't the energy to try and explain. And the temptation to just say nothing, to let someone else deal with it, was too much. So I said nothing.

'Your video's doing well,' was the second surprising thing she said.

'What do you mean?'

'It's on YouTube, the third most watched video on there. It's gone viral. Punkawalla have been offered a recording contract for the song you used.'

'Why would anyone want to watch the video? It was just supposed to be for people at work.'

She stopped and turned to me, the early morning sun behind me giving her beautiful face a glow full of life, of the promise of spring. That face, lit just like that, would cover *Vogue* soon.

'They want to watch it because it's good, Dan.'

'Bryan, my name's Bryan.'

She whacked my arm. 'Your name's not important, Dan, or Bryan, or whatever. It's you. It's you, not who you pretend to be.'

She wasn't expressing herself very well, but I think

I got what she meant.

'People aren't interested in that video because of what you did, they're watching it because you've got talent. You created a slick, attractive product and people want that.'

I thought this over for a while as we walked on. Then I shook my head.

'It's not supposed to be like this.'

'Well that's the way it is,' she replied. Then she stopped me again. A duck squabbled with its mate in the slow-moving river to our right.

'It's just . . .'

'What? It's just what?' she snapped, exasperated.

'I was supposed to face up to my . . . to the consequences of what I'd done. That was the decision I made in Paris. When it all fell down.'

She watched me sideways as we stepped along the muddy towpath. I went on.

'That's why I made the video, not to show off what a great talent I am, or to reveal the dark underbelly of the TV industry.'

The sun leaked out from behind a grey splodge of a cloud. I squinted.

'It was a confession,' I said, realising I was sounding a bit whiny, 'an admission of guilt. I wanted to make sure I couldn't wriggle out of it.'

'Hang on,' she said. 'You want to be arrested? You want to have debts over your head for the next ten years? You're an idiot.'

'Maybe,' I said. 'But it looks like I'll get away without even a slap on the wrist. I might even be rewarded.'

We walked on in silence for a bit.

'I understand,' she said, eventually.

'Keep in touch, yeah?' I said as we stood on the train platform. She was headed back to London, and from there, on to New York where she was back on the catwalk for D&G.

She looked at me and smiled. 'I'm not a postcard kind of girl,' she said.

'Me neither,' I agreed.

'When you're a famous movie director though you can look me up,' she said and winked.

The train arrived, doors hissing open.

'So you can get into my film?' I said arching an eyebrow.

'No, so you can get into my knickers,' she laughed and kissed me. And suddenly it was all real again for a minute.

But then she was gone. I felt an odd mixture of emotions as I walked back to the house. I couldn't make sense of it all. So I stopped trying for a bit and went up to my bedroom with a pack of Mum's cigarettes she thought she'd had well-hidden.

Eventually I steeled my nerve and called Amelie.

'Dan who?' she said sniffily.

'I'm sorry I didn't call, I've been a bit messed up.'

'I know, Dan, and I understand.'

Amelie told me she'd spoken to her friend Kate in the accounts department and that GTV had got Hans to pay for the hotel damage. Katerina had covered the rest. The video was never mentioned, or at least not by management. It looked like they were trying to forget the whole thing. I was relieved, and disappointed at the same time.

'Oh, one more thing,' Amelie said, before I hung up. 'Piers wanted your number. Something about a TV show set in a pub?'

I told her to give him this number and hung up, after promising to call again once I'd got my act together. I sat and thought these new developments over. Was Piers going to make the show? Was he going to credit me? Or better yet, ask me to work on the project? Was I to benefit from my fraud? My deception? Something didn't feel right. I felt as though people didn't fully appreciate what an arse I'd been. I had to explain.

The phone call came that day when I got home.

'Who? Dan? No, no Dan here,' clunk.

Whoops.

'Oh that might be for me, Mum.'

'No, they asked for Dan.'

'Yeah, sure, if they call back it's for me, OK?'

But I wished I'd stayed Bryan by the end of the day. The call turned out to be from some journalist.

'Hello, is that Dan Lewis?'

'Who's asking?'

'I'm a journalist with *Sunday Style* magazine – it comes with the *Courier*, on a Sunday. I'm writing an article and I wondered if I could talk to you.'

'What about?'

'Liarliar? It was you who made that web documentary, wasn't it? You posted it on—'

But I hung up.

My stomach churned. How had this woman found me? What did this mean? Had GTV called the police? Were they pressing charges? But Katerina had cleared the debts. My debts.

The phone rang again and I unplugged it. Mum never got any calls anyway.

But then my mobile went! How the hell had she got that number? I ran upstairs and dragged it out of the bag I'd brought back from London and not bothered to unpack yet.

'Hello?'

'Hi, Dan . . .'

It was her again.

'How did you get this number?'

'I . . . My . . . Actually, that's not really important. What I wanted to ask was – would you mind if I came to see you?

I made the mistake of pausing for a second and she carried on.

'Is that OK? Great. I'll be there at 10 a.m. tomorrow.'

'What? No . . .' But she'd hung up.

I lay awake most of the night, worrying about it. I told myself a thousand times I wasn't going to talk to her, but then argued against myself. This was my opportunity to explain what I'd intended with the film. It was important. If the film didn't say what I wanted, what I needed, it to say, then not only was the real story not being told, but once again I was benefiting under false pretences. But why was she interested? I knew this wasn't a huge story, which was presumably why only a young reporter would be interested. All the juicy stories were fought over by the more experienced hacks. She was digging here in the hope of finding something. Perhaps some connection to Katerina.

When I heard the cheesy bell chimes on the door go just before 10 a.m. the next morning, I had made up my mind to send her away with a flea in each ear. I shoved my cereal bowl aside roughly and stomped to the door.

'Hi? Are you Dan?'

She was pretty. And nice-looking. I'd hoped for some old haggard tabloid harpy I could be horrible to. It's really hard for guys to be nasty to pretty girls, especially when they smile like this girl was smiling.

'No, I mean yes, I mean, well really no, my name's Bryan, but . . . look I don't want to talk to you.'

'Oh.' She looked crestfallen. 'I've come all this way.'

'I'm sorry,' I said. I nearly gave in then, but stiffened my resolve. She worked for a Sunday newspaper for Christ's sake, was she really going to write the story the way I wanted? Even if she would, her editor would change it all to make it more salacious. They'd dig up all the names and places and then the shit would really hit the fan, but for the wrong reasons. It wouldn't be me who'd get humiliated, it'd be Amelie, Edie Morgan, Rashid. I didn't care about Waters but he'd bring the others down with him.

No this wasn't the right way to do it.

'No,' I said firmly and went to close the door.

But she stopped me. She jammed herself into the doorway so I'd be slamming the door in her face. Clever technique. Perhaps she did doorstepping for the Tory party in her spare time. She was scribbling on the margin of a magazine.

'Take this,' she said. 'It's got my name and number. Please?'

I could see desperation in her eyes. I saw myself in there. Hope, fear, terror even, at the big bad world she was hoping to make her way in. She was young. She needed this. She needed a step up, a helping hand, a foot in the door.

But why did it have to be *my* door?

I took the magazine and made sure I got her out of the door then went upstairs to think.

An hour later, I set up the trusty camcorder, battered and scratched by its adventures in Paris and London but still working fine. I sat before it and began to record a new film. This time, the whole story. With nothing left out. And with clear instructions as to who should be held responsible.

It is the story I've just told you. And now it ends.

Int. Day. Dan's room. He ejects a disk from a computer and drops it into a Jiffy bag, which he seals. He picks up a pen and, referring to the inside page of a magazine, writes on the parcel. Cut to close-up of Jiffy bag. Label reads:

Becky Dunford
Sunday Style
1 Canada Square
Canary Wharf
London E14 5XX

Turn over to read the

consequence

of this story...

Prologue

Waiting, waiting, waiting. It felt like I was waiting for my life to happen. Waiting to take my A-levels, waiting to leave school and go to uni, waiting to make my own way (without my parents' interference), waiting to discover someone I liked enough to go out with for more than two weeks.

I thought it was all about to start when I found The Story. The one about the runner who pretended he was a TV hotshot and landed up with debts everywhere because he was trying to impress some wannabe model. Dan Lewis's story. It even got into the paper – the real paper, not just the Sunday women's magazine supplement where I was doing my summer work placement. I thought I was going to explode, I was so ecstatic. An article I'd written (with a little help) was in the national press. Can you believe it? My friend Sally messaged me a photo from the newsagent round the corner from her house. Her finger was pointing to my name on the page: 'By Becky Dunford.'

'Fraudster tells all to our rookie reporter,' the *Courier* had gushed.

And then . . . nothing much changed. After a few days of

everyone congratulating me, it was back pretty much to how it was before. At the *Courier* I was still the work experience girl, sorting out a mess of lipsticks and concealers for the Beauty Editor. Had I just blown the beginning of my new life? Had it stalled before it even started?

Of course, I had three more weeks left on a placement that most girls (and some boys) would kill for, and I meant to make the most of them. But why bronze is the new silver and all those stories about people's beautiful homes and how you can look twenty when you're actually forty-two . . . they really aren't me. I'm more Orla Guerin than Orla Kiely. (That's the line I've been practising for when I find my perfect boyfriend material – although Sally rather spoilt things by pointing out that it will probably be wasted on most straight boys. Orly-who? And whatsa-Keeley?)

I needed to get myself noticed by the news desk – and do it so well that this time they wouldn't forget me again after my fifteen minutes. But how was I going to do that?

My train dragged itself into Swindon station. I wanted it to go faster, hurrying me to London after a weekend in dull, safe Bath.

Don't get me wrong – I love Bath. World Heritage Site and all that. It's beautiful to look at (or most of it is, anyway), with its Georgian terraces and the green hills behind. It's great when you're a kid and want to run around in fields and play hide-and-seek and make dens. But hanging out in the town gets boring as soon as you're past, like, eleven years old. Unless, of course, there's a tourist group to eye up with some cool-looking Italian boys who might take you to a café and talk about film or books or really anything that's Not Rugby. (I can't stand rugby.)

But I wanted more. Or something else. Something faster, and bigger, with more excitement and more possibilities. London. That's what I wanted. London, and to be a proper journalist, and to 'see the world'.

I was on the Monday morning 9.12 – the rush-hour was over but there were still some business people on their way to meetings, with their jackets folded neatly next to them. Unusually for the past few weeks, my dad wasn't with me; he's an MP and he had some 'constituency business' this morning. I had a seat by the window, at one of the tables. I was curled up with my iPod and the latest downloads and watching the countryside blur past. In one field a couple of deer were munching grass or leaves; I've seen plenty of deer from the window now that I'm a regular commuter. Across from me a guy in a striped shirt was tapping on his laptop, stopping now and again to answer his mobile. He was loud and glossy and his aftershave was too strong. He had to be an estate agent.

Outside the sun was blazing down, evaporating the early morning rain. Last month, during my exams, had been a heatwave, and another was predicted. But the July weather so far had been wet and disappointing. I'd wanted a steamy summer in London – sunbathing in the park, ice-cream melting over my hands (and the hands of someone I might happen to meet?).

Along the carriage was a group about my age. Boys showing off and girls giggling. I could just about see this one boy with dark hair and a sort of I'm-just-into-my-music look, holding himself slightly apart as he listened through his headphones (the kind that cover your whole ear). He wasn't a geeky type. His haircut was too trendy. He looked as though he could be one of those moody and mean types. I couldn't decide if I disliked him on sight or fancied him. But I couldn't take my eyes off him. Then his gaze flickered over in my direction and I suddenly became all shy and quickly looked out of the window to pretend that I hadn't been staring. And then slid my eyes back when he turned away again.

Which meant that I missed the beginning of The Conversation . . .

Read the first book in the exciting **Consequences series**

Katie's landed a job as nanny to the kids of Britain's most notorious couple. He's a gorgeous premier footballer, she's a volatile ex-dancer. And Katie's all set for a life in the spotlight. But she didn't factor in the downside to her job. The confidentiality clause, the truth behind the celebrity marriage, and the skeletons hiding in the designer wardrobe Somebody's got a sad, dark secret just waiting to come out Has Katie got it in her to betray it – or will someone else beat her to it?

Natalie's been taking photographs since she got her first camera as a kid. She belongs behind a camera, and she wants to make it big – as big as Annie Leibowitz, her all-time heroine. Then Natalie takes the photograph that will change her life. It will bring her fame, money and more 'exposure' than she ever dreamed of. But you know what they say about fame If you're lucky you'll get your 15 seconds, use it. Use it well...

Read the third book in the exciting **Consequences series**

No one is more surprised than Jen Jones when top model scout Corinne Taylor flags her down in Top Shop and hands over her business card. Before she knows it Jen is in runway heaven, heading for the cover of Vogue. She is only too happy to be shot of school and all the losers who think she looks 'weird'. But not Stevie. Jen could never leave Stevie behind He's always been her soul mate, her rock. Nothing could possibly drive them apart ...could it?